THREE DAYS

WENDY SMITH

Edited by
LAUREN CLARKE

Cover Design by
MOSS DESIGNS

All rights reserved. No part of this book may be reproduced or transmitted in any form, including electronic or mechanical, without written permission from the publisher, except in the case of brief quotations embodied in critical articles or reviews.

This is a work of fiction. Names, characters, businesses, places, events, and incidents are either the products of the author's imagination or used in a fictitious manner. Any resemblance to actual persons, living or dead, or actual events is purely coincidental. Ariadne Wayne is in no way affiliated with any brands, songs, musicians or artists mentioned in this book.

* Content warning - Early pregnancy loss, domestic violence

© Wendy Smith 2014

❋ Created with Vellum

BLURB

He's rebuilding his life after hitting rock bottom. She's the whirlwind he can't help but fall for.

Andrew's wife died in his arms. Overwhelming grief destroyed him, leading to him committing a crime during his breakdown. After three years in prison, he has nothing and desperately needs to start a new life.

The last thing he expects to find is love. But Maddy has her own past to deal with before they can move forward together.

ONE

I NEVER MEANT to hurt her.

That sounds crazy when I think of what I put Rowan through.

None of it made sense until so much later. When I sat in the prison cell, the realisation of what I'd done hit me like a freight train. Consumed with thoughts of getting her back, I'd wanted to reset time, take us back to the way things used to be. Charlie's death had made that impossible.

Now, I sat in the same cell I'd inhabited for these past three years, thinking about how to put things right. Memories of what I did haunted me. I still dreamed of a happier time, when Charlie, Rowan and I were three musketeers. Charlie was dead, and even being friends with Rowan was so far out of my reach that nothing would ever be the same.

I looked around the walls, drab, that same uniform grey the whole damn building was painted in. These were the walls I'd stared at so many times, wondering how my life could have gone if I had done things differently. It was when I closed my eyes that the memories came flooding back.

Charlie, my beautiful blue-eyed girl. The one who'd committed to love me every day of my life; the one I'd let down so badly. It wasn't that I had any doubts, but seeing Rowan with another man had left me on edge. I didn't know I'd wanted her until I couldn't have her.

I was stupid, immature, desperate, and I'd lost the two people who meant the most to me in the whole world.

Standing, I took one last look around the cell. I wouldn't miss this place, and yet I'd learned so much about myself while sitting inside these walls.

It was time to get out of here.

With all formalities aside, I made my way to the gate, pausing to look around the big, almost empty car park leading to the road. I shivered. *Never coming back here again.*

My parents stood either side of the car, waiting. At sight of me, Mum yelped, and ran, throwing her arms around me and hugging me tight. "Let's go home," she whispered.

BEFORE ALL THIS, I'd had a good job, a good life. Now, I had to start again, find a way to exist with a criminal record for this crazy thing I'd done. I couldn't imagine doing it now; the guilt was overwhelming at times. To take Rowan away from her family had been cruel, but at the time, I hadn't been able to see past my grief and confusion.

Charlie. I still dreamed of Charlie. Our wedding day was blighted by my resentment over Kyle, Rowan's date. My bride had walked down the aisle, covered in satin and lace, and all I could see was Kyle, his arms wrapped around Rowan as if he possessed her.

I'd been more upset when Rowan broke off our friendship than I let on, pretended to be indifferent rather than let her see just how deeply it affected me. We'd been inseparable when we were younger; suddenly not having her in my life had wrecked me.

The car ride was long, and my thoughts turned to how we used to travel in this same car all those years ago, along this same road. My dad had this huge sentimental attachment to the old HQ Holden he drove, and prided himself on keeping it going for all this time. Rowan, Charlie and I would all sit together in the big backseat, Charlie and I often teasing Rowan about the way she fell asleep on every long journey.

I closed my eyes, unable to count the number of times I'd found her slumped over, held only by a lap belt, her head on my lap as she dozed. Sometimes, when no one was looking, I'd stroke her hair and wonder what life would bring us. The first girl I ever kissed; the first girl to make sense.

"Shit. We shouldn't have come this way," said Dad, waking me out of my daydream. The long, rural road took us past the place where my parents used to own a beach house, the last place I saw Rowan.

"It's okay, Dad," I said, gazing out the window. Her screams, police, crashing in and taking her away, saving her from me—her former best friend.

"I'm sorry, Andrew. I know this must be upsetting for you," he said, pressing his foot to the accelerator as if trying to get away as quickly as possible.

"I just have to live with it," I said. I looked up at the rear-view mirror, catching his eye, seeing the sorrow in his expression. He didn't want to make me relive what I'd done, but I would never stop, regardless of his actions.

"Sweetheart, we know you're not a bad person. You just did a bad thing," Mum said.

I nodded. That had to be the understatement of the year, but somehow it was reassuring.

WE WENT past the orchard where Rowan's parents lived as we drew close to home. The big, old white house stood high among the trees. Every place was steeped in memories of our childhood, and despite my parents trying to take care of me, I wondered how long it would be before I had to leave to stop myself drowning in them.

Rowan's father was out by the boundary, and waved at Mum and Dad as we went past. At least my actions hadn't screwed the friendship Mum and Dad had with Rowan's parents, but I knew it had been strained for a while.

Mum was a stickler for the garden being neat and tidy. The grounds at home were immaculate, as always. The house still looked new, thanks to my father's sometimes obsessive cleaning of it. They'd lived in this place for thirty years, and you could have sworn it had just been built.

My room was still the same as it had been when I lived here. Back before Charlie and I got together, before the mess that followed. The single bed below the window, the window I used to climb out to run down the road and see Charlie, or in the other direction to see Rowan.

In the corner were some boxes. I recognised them from my old apartment. We'd packed it up before I'd gone inside, and I'd forgotten they were there.

I opened the first one, pulling out a photo of Charlie and I. It was one of our engagement photos, and she was beaming, the love radiating off her like rays of the sun. There I was, gazing adoringly at her. If only things had stayed that simple.

The longer I looked, the closer I came to tears, the weight of my grief overwhelming me as if it were happening all over again. I had so many regrets about the past, but none about loving Charlie.

I had to start a new life, and I had no idea how. All I knew was that I was alone, and I had to deal with it without flipping out again. Doing it once had cost me far too much.

It cost me everything.

TWO

I COULDN'T STAY.

So many memories surrounded me back home. Everywhere I went reminded me of Charlie. I couldn't even face her gravestone, so ashamed of my behaviour. She'd been gone three weeks when I'd made a move on Rowan, pushing myself on her even though I knew she was with Kyle. My grief so fresh, I'd reached out to the one person who I thought could bring me comfort, and nearly ruined her life.

I could barely remember what I was thinking at that time—that's how screwed up I'd been. The last thing I'd needed was to immerse myself in the past when what I needed to do was find the future.

Everything around me screamed of Charlie. My old room, where we'd played as children. Her old house, just down the road. I couldn't even go to see Charlie's parents—my pain over losing her was still so raw. I'd let them down when I'd kidnapped Rowan, their hearts had been as broken as my own parents. Coming home had been like ripping the Band-Aid off. What was I thinking?

Then, there were the dreams ...

"I don't know what your issue is with Kyle, but you can't interfere

in Rowan's life. I know you want to protect her from anything bad happening, but he obviously cares about her and I can't have you push her away when I just got her back." Charlie's chest rose and fell hard and fast as she screamed the words.

"And whose fault is that?" I yelled back. "I wanted to tell her about us, let her down gently. You were always the one against telling her."

"I'll always regret that. I missed her so much, Andrew. What I don't want now is for you to upset and estrange her."

I shook my head in frustration. "Why didn't you ask her to be part of the wedding party?"

Her face had reddened in anger; now the colour drained from her cheeks. "I always promised my sisters they'd be my bridesmaids."

"You're worried about me pushing her away? Don't you think she might feel used by you? She helped you with so much wedding prep, and you didn't include her."

Tears sprung up in her eyes. I was being mean and I knew it, but this argument was decidedly one-sided. We'd been in it together, hiding our love from our best friend because we both knew it would hurt her. Married three days and we were further apart than we had been for so very long.

I hated myself for hurting her when I loved her more than anything. Hated that I was torn over Rowan. Hated that I'd lost both of them.

I SAT on the back step as Dad washed his car. That thing was so precious to him, he lovingly soaped the car up with a sponge. It was like watching a man shower with the woman he loved and brought a smile to my lips as the suds slid down the drive and into the drain on the street. Both he and Mum were so fastidious about everything. He kept cleaning the same spot over and over again, trying to get some invisible dirt off. I still couldn't see it.

Mum opened the door behind me. "Want a coffee, love?" she asked.

I nodded, turning to look up at her. "That'd be great. Thanks."

"What are you going to do now?"

I shrugged, turning back to watch Dad, not wanting to talk. If only the water could wash away this lost feeling. What I needed was something to anchor me, something secure to help me back. I had some ideas, just hadn't formed a plan.

"Didn't you think about it?" she pressed on.

"I didn't think of anything else. It just all seemed pointless without Charlie." I stood. She moved out of the way as I came back inside the house, and followed me into the living room where her own coffee sat on a coaster on the table.

She disappeared, returning a few moments later with a cup. I placed mine beside it with no coaster. Some stupid little act of rebellion with no idea what I was fighting.

"Oh, Andrew." She sighed, lifting the cup to place a coaster under it.

"Everything feels like a waste of time," I said. I sat back on the couch, lifting my feet to rest on the table. She sighed again.

"You have to make a fresh start. Why don't you work for your dad for a while, save some money?"

I shrugged. "Because if I'm making a fresh start I can't be here. Everything around here reminds me of Charlie. If I go to the end of the driveway and turn right, I'll end up going past her parents' place; if I turn left, I'll go past Rowan's. I love you guys, but I'm already feeling trapped just by coming home."

She frowned, even though my words weren't aimed at her. It was this place, not them.

"I don't understand. Why would memories of Charlie cause you issues?"

I shook my head. "Seriously? It was Charlie's death that did this to me. It broke me, Mum. Stopped me from seeing all reason, led to this."

A vibrant red spread across her cheeks, and she lowered her eyes to avert my gaze. "Sorry. I didn't even think of it that way."

"What I want is to turn back the clock, back to that day, make things better between us."

She looked up, pursing her lips. If I knew her at all, she was wondering whether to say something else.

"What is it, Mum?"

"What happened? I never asked you what happened."

Dad had, Dad and Rowan and the police in the end. Not Mum. She had sat there quietly, supporting me through it all. I took my feet off the table, leaning forward to talk to her.

"Charlie was so sheltered growing up. Her parents might as well have put her in a plastic bubble at times. I just never thought after all that time it would happen to her." I sucked in a deep breath. "We chose our honeymoon spot because Charlie wanted to try something new. Trees and flowers and sunshine surrounded us, and she loved every second. Right at the end, our argument was meaningless. Her eyes told me how she felt, just as they always did, and all I saw was love."

Mum's eyes shone, and she closed them as the tears rolled down her cheeks.

"She was upset, and she ran. We were in the wrong place, and too far from anywhere to get help in time. But, I loved her, Mum. I might have got confused about seeing Rowan with Kyle, but I loved Charlie. We would have been happy together and gotten through it. And then none of this would have happened. I miss her so much."

I buried my face in my hands, hiding the tears that now flowed. Charlie and I had been so happy and in love. If I could, I'd redo everything differently, be happy for Rowan instead of weirding out about her being with another guy. When she'd walked away from Charlie and I, I'd missed her, but seeing her with someone else had made me crazy.

"I'm sorry, love. I know you loved Charlie; it was obvious when you two were together. I didn't mean to upset you."

"It's okay," I said. "You look pretty upset too."

"You were all my children. I loved the three of you, and it hurts that Charlie is gone and Rowan can't be a part of our lives. Her mother gives me updates from time to time, but it's not the same."

"I just hope she's happy."

Mum smiled. "That man of hers has made her very happy. I have a Christmas card somewhere with a photo of the three of them. Rowan has a beautiful little girl."

I swallowed down my guilt about that girl. Baby Mia. She was four months old when I abducted her mother and took her away without a thought about her. I knew of her existence; I'd visited Rowan in the hospital the day after her birth, and it was thoughts of her that tormented me the most.

"I'll get it." She stood, shuffling off up the hallway. I wasn't even sure if I wanted to see it.

Within minutes she returned, waving it at me, excited to find it.

There was Rowan. Her smile made my heart ache as I suffered pangs of missing her. Her presence had always been reassuring; she had this calmness about her that I'd never found in anyone else.

She stood in front of Kyle, his arms wrapped around her protectively. After what I did, he probably kept her as close as possible.

In front of them both stood Mia—she must be older than three by now. She looked so much like her mother, but I could see her father in her too. She wore a Santa hat, and had a grin on her face a mile wide, one she shared with her parents. They couldn't look any happier.

Seeing them that way made me feel warm inside. Rowan had found true love and happiness.

I just needed to find myself.

THREE

ANOTHER NIGHT, another dream.

They returned with the vengeance of an abandoned lover. When I was inside, the dreams had faded, not entirely leaving me, but letting me get some sleep. Now, every night for the past five I'd woken in a sweat, dreaming of the woman I'd loved, the one I'd sworn to love forever.

"I'm leaving," I told Mum and Dad in the morning.

Mum gaped; hell, she was probably scared I'd lose the plot again. Dad just nodded as if he could see inside my head, as if he knew what I was going through.

"Where are you going to go?"

"Maybe I'll see if I can get my old job back." I closed my eyes, not wanting to see their faces, judging me without realising.

"That puts you back near Rowan," Mum said.

"And near my counsellor, who I'll be seeing once a month anyway. There's a boarding house not too far from him that accepts people like me, so the rent is cheaper than finding a place of my own. Once I'm working, I'll find an apartment or something."

"You have it all planned out," she whispered.

"I love you, Mum, but this isn't working. I need to do what's best for me right now."

I ENJOYED BEING on the road two days later, even if it was only to go for a drive to the local mall. My car had sat in the garage at Mum and Dad's place while I'd been inside, and Dad had kept it maintained for my return.

The sound of the engine purring gave me such a feeling of freedom before I'd even driven out the door. I could go anywhere, do anything—it was like having some of my power given back to me.

"It's gassed up. I did it before we left. Figured you might like to go for a drive and get some fresh air. Lord knows you'll be keen on that."

I grinned. "You read my mind."

He fished out his wallet, handing me some notes. "Go into town, buy yourself what you need. I know you have your savings in the bank, but you'll have to organise cards and things. Just be free, Andrew."

"Thanks, Dad."

I revved the engine. God, this felt good. Slowly, I moved towards the street, waving at Dad as I moved. At the end of the driveway I had to decide which way to go. I chose Charlie's way.

My heart was in my throat as I drove past, slowing to take a look. They'd painted the house. It was no longer a pale beige, but a light blue—Charlie's favourite colour. I didn't have to ask to know that this was a tribute to her.

I kept going until I hit the shopping mall, parking the car and walking to the stores. It had been three years since I'd been shopping, since I'd been able to look at this and choose what I wanted. The simple things meant more than anything else. Just walking through clothing stories, the feel of the fabric beneath my fingers—buying something nice was so indulgent.

And still I thought of Charlie.

She'd done a lot of my clothes shopping. Nothing got past without her approval. We'd known each other so well and for so long; she knew my tastes and fitted them in with hers. I would have worn a hessian sack if she'd asked me to.

I walked out towards the bookshop. Maybe a good paperback would keep me preoccupied, if only for a while. Turning the last corner, I nearly ran into Rowan's mother coming the other way.

The colour drained from her face as she saw me.

"I'm sorry, Mrs Taylor. Going too fast."

She stood for a moment, just looking at me. I don't think she knew what to say. Taking a deep breath, she forced the words out. "Oh, Andrew. Are you home now?"

"For the moment. I need to find a job, and I've got to go back for counselling sessions so I won't be sticking around here for long."

She gulped. All the years I'd known her she'd never been good at hiding her feelings.

"So you'll be around Rowan?"

"In the same city, but not around her. I have to find my feet."

Uncertainty crossed her face. I didn't have to ask what she was worried about.

"I won't go anywhere near her. What I did was wrong, and I was out of my mind when I did it. I'm in control now."

She seemed to take in my words, nodding. I'd been as close to this woman as my own mother at one time. Now we were like strangers, and it was all my fault. When I'd been away, I hadn't thought that much about her. Now I saw her, I missed her.

"Mrs Taylor, I'm okay now. Want to go for coffee? We can talk some more about it if you'd like to."

"I don't know if I can," she whispered.

"I understand. I'll be at Mum and Dad's for a few more days if you want to talk." She wouldn't come; I already knew that. Of course her loyalty was to Rowan. Rowan's parents adored her; I'd be the last person she'd want to hang out with.

She nodded, moving past me without saying another word. I

watched as she disappeared into the distance, glad she was by herself. Rowan's father would probably have thumped me.

I wouldn't have blamed him.

"YOU'RE BROODING," Mum said, as she cleared the dinner plates off the table. "You haven't said a word since you got home."

"I'll do that, Mum," I said, standing and taking the plates from her hands.

"I'm worried about you."

"You're always worried about me."

She sighed. "This is about you leaving, isn't it?"

I walked to the sink, and starting running the water to wash the dishes.

"I ran into Mrs Taylor at the mall today," I said, turning to look at her. She frowned, leaning against the kitchen counter as if needing it for support.

"I've got to go, Mum. At the very least I have to try to prove myself, and show everyone that I'm not the same man I used to be."

Moving the dishes into the water, I grabbed the scrubbing brush and started to clean. Mum just stood there, watching as I moved around, doing both the washing and drying. Her eyes bore through me, as she followed my every move, looking pensive.

"I'm scared, Andrew," she said softly.

"Scared of what?"

"That it'll all just get too much for you again."

I dried my hands on the towel, and gripped her arms. "This is why I need to prove myself. If even you think I'm going to snap again, it shows what an uphill battle I have."

"You can't go near her. You can't."

"Mum," I said, meaning what was about to come out of my mouth. "I won't."

FOUR

I SPENT hours in a car by myself with nothing but the radio to keep my company. I'd switched to some station playing 70s songs, lured by the old songs we used to listen to out of Charlie's father's vinyl collection.

Drawn to the music despite the need to take a break from my memories, I sang along with the songs I never really liked back then. For her.

I'd left in the dark. It felt like sneaking away leaving at an early hour, but I had said my goodbyes and just wanted to get on the road and away. Running into Rowan's mother had been the final push for me to go.

As the sun rose, I realised I hadn't seen this for so very long. The first morning of our honeymoon, we'd been in bed and watched the light start filtering through the curtains, the romance of the moment not missed by either of us.

Stop it. You have to stop living in the past.

The woman who ran the boarding house had agreed to meet me to discuss a possible tenancy. It was a halfway house for former prison inmates. I'd be surrounded by others who might just have similar experiences to me. She was notoriously careful about whom she let live there, and I couldn't blame her.

My counsellor, Steve, warned me she might not let me in. She didn't like men who were violent in any way, particularly with women, and he was concerned she would see me in that light. When he'd said that, my stomach began to ache. The thought of people seeing me as an abuser stung, but I hadn't exactly treated Rowan right.

I didn't want to intrude too early, so I stopped at a cafe. When the coffee arrived, I took in the aroma, letting it permeate my senses. Mum and Dad drank instant, but there was nothing like a real coffee, brewed and prepared just the way I liked it. Somewhere, packed away with all my things in Mum and Dad's garage, was a coffee machine. There were too many boxes to pack in my car, so I'd left it behind for the moment.

Once you're settled, you can have this every day.

The little things were what made me happy.

I RETURNED.

To the park where Kyle told me to leave his wife alone, to the park where I watched her so many times walking her baby, talking to her, singing to her. The gentle lullaby would carry through the air, further than I think Rowan ever thought it would. She would have been mortified if she'd realised. It calmed me as it did the baby, bringing me back to the old days when she'd loved me and I hadn't done anything about it because I didn't know I'd loved her too.

I ducked behind a tree when I spotted them walking down the path. Rowan smiled and laughed, wrapping her arm around Kyle and resting her head on his shoulder as they strolled, their little girl holding her mother's hand, skipping as she went. So much like Rowan, but so confident at the same time. Not shy and retiring like her mother had been.

Seeing her again brought me a sense of calm, but my chest ached at the thought of that being mine. If I had not been such an idiot, seen what I needed to far too late. Now, there was no chance of being close to her, not even as a friend.

"Mummy, pick me up," the little girl screeched. I closed my eyes at the sound; she could have been my child if I hadn't screwed things up.

"Mia, come here." I head Kyle's voice. "Mummy can't pick you up right now. But, if you want, you can ride on my shoulders."

I peeked around the tree, and watched as he scooped the little girl up, swinging her onto his shoulders as she squealed with laughter. Rowan smiled, her hand resting on her stomach as I realised why she couldn't pick up her daughter.

Waiting until they were out of sight, I ran back to the car. I couldn't do this again. As much as I wanted to say I was sorry, if I got caught approaching her, I'd be back inside as quick as I could blink.

She was happy, and with the man she adored. I still remembered her begging me to let her go home, while I tried so hard to get her to see how she needed to leave him and be with me.

I have no idea what I'd been thinking, so obsessed with convincing her to leave him and be with me. All rational thought was left behind as she'd called out for help, and I'd bound her wrists together with tape, making sure the child locks were set on the back doors so she couldn't get out of the car.

She'd still tried to fight, until I bound her feet together, and she was left lying on the backseat, weeping and begging me to return her to her family. It was like I hadn't heard her words. There was only one place we could go.

With time and clarity, my actions weighed heavily on me. How could I leave that little baby all alone in the house? While Kyle was there, I hit him with the heaviest object I could lay my hands on quickly, and he went down hard.

For all I knew at the time, I could have killed him.

My hands gripped the steering wheel of the car, squeezing it until my knuckles turned white. I couldn't reconcile the way I'd acted back then to myself; that was not the way I behaved. And yet, for those few days, I had gone crazy with needing her to listen to me, being blind to everything else.

I didn't know why I'd come here. The sense of familiarity, perhaps. She used to come here every day with Mia around the same time, but I'd had no idea she'd be there today. I thought I'd be able to walk around, and feel her presence in the wind.

So stupid.

Time to go and see this place I'd be staying at.

Time to start again.

FIVE

THE BOARDING HOUSE WAS A BIG, old, Victorian manor. Whitewashed, but greyed with dirt, the whole place looked run down, moss growing on the walls at the base where water leaked. How this place was still standing, I had no idea. But, it was cheap.

I walked into the large lobby area, looking down at the polished hardwood floors that gave the interior of the house a much newer look than the exterior. They looked maintained, even if nothing else did.

I took a look at my surroundings. A large communal area was on the left of me, with couches and chairs, all pretty threadbare. Two men sat on a old red leather couch, cracked with the stuffing coming out in tufts. They were watching the large flat-screen on the wall. Straight ahead was a big, sweeping staircase and around the side of that, a corridor seemed to lead out the back, where I assumed the rooms to rent were.

There was just one door on the right, and there was a sign attached to it that read *Rental Enquiries Here*.

Approaching it, I knocked on the door. The facade of the tidy entrance fell apart as I felt the softness of the wood under my fist. It wouldn't take much to put a hole in it.

A woman opened the door. I guessed she was about fifty. She had greying hair, but wore skin-tight jeans and a Metallica T-shirt. She looked me up and down, raising an eyebrow before smiling.

"Hi," she said. I knew that expression. Before Charlie, I'd never had any trouble getting girls interested, and that was the look.

"Hi. I'm Andrew Carmichael. I called about the room?"

"Of course. I'm Carly Jones. Please, come in." She stood back, ushering me into the small area behind her. The temperature rose as I entered, a small heater going in the corner. It wasn't that cold, but I had my doubts about whether the place was insulated. In the corner was a display case with trophy after trophy, a bookcase against one wall with what looked like a ton of old books on display, a couch in the middle of the room, and a small television in the corner. Very cosy.

She pointed to the couch, and I sat. From a door leading to what I assumed was the kitchen, the scent of meat told me she probably had been cooking a casserole all day, and my mouth watered at the thought. It was just like being at home, and even after just coming from Mum and Dad's, I had a pang of homesickness.

"I'm a bit choosy about whom I let live here, as I've told you," she said, sitting next to me. "But, I heard about your wife, and a part of me got it. I can't pretend I understand your crime, but no one should have to lose someone they love, not as young as you two were. You deserve a fresh start, Andrew. At least, that's what I think."

I nodded. Every word she said made sense.

"Thanks, Carly."

"We'll go up in a minute, but this used to be a motel, so the rooms are more fully-contained units. As I explained the rooms are furnished, but you're more than welcome to move your own things in. The main room has some furniture, and there's a bench with a small kitchen area with stove, microwave and fridge. You'll have your own bathroom with shower and toilet, so it's very private. At the same time, we have a large communal lounge down here with a couple of

TVs and couches. It's not The Ritz, but it's warm, dry, comfortable and clean."

I let out the breath I'd been holding as she described the place. It all sounded great to me, especially the privacy. I wanted to be out among people, but I didn't want to be surrounded either. This would be a great place to gather my thoughts and get my shit together. Once I found a job that paid enough, I could move on and get a place of my own.

"You look relieved." She smiled at me, more like a mother than someone who was interested five minutes ago.

"I'm just glad to find somewhere to live. I don't think this will be easy, but this is one less thing to worry about."

She nodded. "That's what we're here for. I just need you to take a look at the rental form, and if you're ready we can go and take a look at the room."

"Sure."

"There's no rush, either. If you need to stay tonight and read it all over, take your time and we can talk some more tomorrow."

She handed me the papers and a pen, and I looked down at the words, which suddenly seemed like a lot to take in. This was what being a grown-up was all about.

"It's a big adjustment, being back out. Hopefully this is a start."

"I really appreciate it, Carly. To be honest I had no idea where to start. All I knew was that I couldn't stay with my parents and go to work for my dad. That was the easy option. I need to work this out for me."

She smiled, patting me on the shoulder. "Good for you. Come on, let's take a look at that room."

I followed her out to the stairs, and she led me down a corridor at the top. What she was doing here for these people, including me was amazing. I had to admire her. She clearly did her best to keep the place maintained, but I still had the feeling that if put under closer scrutiny, the place wouldn't be in that good condition under the fresh paint.

The room itself was quite large. There was enough space for me to bring in a television and some of my personal things. The double bed in the corner smelled of fresh linen. It would do until I could afford my own things. She was right about this being a great place to start. It wasn't much, but I could do something with it.

I ran my hand across the bench. It was old, the Formica chipped around the edges, and there was some good cupboard space for groceries. Using some of my savings would help set me up here, and the thought of having all of this at my disposal for the price was just amazing.

"This is great," I said to Carly, "I'm sure you could charge more rent than you do. Though I'm probably shooting myself in the foot, saying that."

"Oh, I know. This old place costs me next to nothing though. My parents left it to me when it was still a motel. I'll admit it needs an overhaul, but I'm happy to help people like you."

I grinned; Carly really was in this for the pleasure of helping people. She was so selfless. "That's awesome. I'll look over the papers tonight and bring some of my stuff in from the car, if that's okay."

"That'll be fine. Do you need a hand bringing things up"

"I'm sure I'll be fine." I walked towards the door, and as I passed her, she handed me the key.

"Come on, we'll ask Bob to help. He's been here forever, and he looks out for all of us."

I cocked my head to look at her. "How long has he been here?"

"Years. He got caught up in a gang in his teens. He was just a kid when he committed armed robbery. Completely harmless, and always feels like he needs to make up for what he did. So, he stays here with us and helps around the place. Such a gentle soul."

I followed her back downstairs and she stopped at a door just back from hers. A man emerged when she knocked. At a guess he was in his early forties, greying hair wild and crazy, and nearly wearing the same clothes she did.

"Bob, this is Andrew. He's coming to stay here for a while. I was wondering if you would help him move some things in from the car."

He lit up at being asked to help, and I couldn't help but smile at the obvious adoration he had for Carly. She seemed completely oblivious.

"Sure thing." He stepped out his door, and offered his hand for me to shake. "Good to meet you, Andrew."

"Likewise. I don't have a lot, but I'd appreciate any help I can get."

He nodded, heading out the door towards my car and I followed. It seemed he kept a real close eye on things, as he knew just which car to go to.

It only took a few trips to bring in everything and when we were finished we stood, looking at the packed boxes. Not much to unpack, but the start of my life was in them.

Boxes, waiting to be unpacked. Charlie had wanted to christen our new bedroom, but I wanted to get the unpacking done. She'd danced and taunted me until I surrendered, following the trail of her clothes to the bed.

I shook my head. It was a relief to have somewhere to live, but at the same time I ached for the life I used to have, the one I'd lost.

"I'm just downstairs if you need anything," Bob said. "Most people around here keep to themselves, but it'd be nice to have someone to talk to from time to time."

I grinned. Making a friend in the first half hour had to be a good sign.

"Sounds great. Thanks for the help."

And then he left me alone in my new home. Free and scared.

I had one more thing to do to say goodbye to the old and hello to the new.

Say sorry.

SIX

I PICKED up and put down the phone maybe twenty times before dialling, taking deep breaths to keep calm when the receptionist answered and I asked for Kyle.

His deep voice came down the line and I closed my eyes, gathering my courage. "Kyle Warner speaking."

For a moment I paused, unable to form words. He had no reason to help me, and every reason to hate me.

"Hello?"

He would hang up if I didn't say something, and I had to get this right. This was the only way I could hope to apologise to Rowan.

"Kyle, it's Andrew Carmichael."

There was silence. He didn't need to say anything for me to realise he was in a state of disbelief. I doubt he ever suspected I would call him, though he must have known I was out of prison.

"Andrew." His calmness was chilling; he wasn't about to show me any emotion.

"I know you have no reason to talk to me, but I need to say some things."

He sighed. "Go ahead."

"I want to apologise to Rowan. The last three years have changed me, and I've sorted all my shit out. She belongs with you; I know that now. I guess I always knew it. I just want to say I'm sorry." I crossed my fingers, hoping that if I grovelled enough, he'd help me. Three years ago, he would have told me where to go.

"Do you have any idea what you're asking me? What you put us all through?" There was nothing in his voice, no anger, and no frustration. Just a flat tone.

"I know what I did, and I don't need anything else but to apologise to Rowan. I'd like to set the record straight on a couple of things, but most of all, I want to say sorry. To you too, and your daughter."

I swear I could hear his brain ticking over.

"I don't want you anywhere near her," he said.

"Totally understand that. We could do this over the phone if we need to. I just want the opportunity to talk, and I'd like to do it face to face."

"Damn it, Andrew. You know it's not up to me, and I'm probably in a no-win situation. If I don't tell her about this and she finds out later, she'll be pissed with me. If I do agree to tell her, she'll think I'm nuts. Hell, it has to be her decision." He sounded conflicted, and I did understand. If anyone had done what I did to my woman, I'd not want her to see him ever again.

"I know this is out of the blue. I've spent the last three years working through all my issues. I'm not expecting friendship, or anything like that."

There was silence again, as I presume he fought with himself over what to do.

"You know how Rowan is about this kind of thing. She'll want to know now you've opened this particular can of worms. Give me your number and I'll talk to her tonight. I can't promise anything, and I can't say which way she's going to go. She's moved on too, but it took her a long time to get over what you did. It took us all a long time to get over it."

The faint glimmer of hope he'd offered began to grow as I gave him my new cell number.

THE FOLLOWING morning the phone rang, and I didn't recognise the number on the caller display.

"Hello?"

"Andrew, it's Kyle."

Lost for words, I opened my mouth to try to force them, but they wouldn't come.

"Hello?" he said.

"Hi. I didn't expect to hear from you so quickly."

"I spoke to Rowan and she's agreed to see you." He sounded flat, almost disappointed.

"Thanks, Kyle. I really appreciate it."

"I'll be right there, so don't even think of trying anything. I'm prepared this time."

Fair enough. I deserved that. I didn't want to see him, but the choice between that and not seeing Rowan was easy.

"I swear I only want to apologise for what I did."

"Is that really all you want?" He wasn't about to let this go.

No. I want my best friend back. I want my wife back. I want everything back the way it was.

"That's all I want," I said.

"We'll be at the park tomorrow morning at ten sharp. We can meet you by the pond. I figured we'd go somewhere public just in case."

I closed my eyes, fighting the urge to take the bait. He would have loved me to have a go at him—, it'd give him an excuse to block Rowan from seeing me. Screw it, she meant more to me than arguing with him.

"I understand."

"Good. And Andrew?"

"Yes?"

"This is going to be the one and only time I let you anywhere near her. Choose your words wisely."

I couldn't get angry with him. He wanted to protect his wife. I understood that so much.

If only I could have done more to protect mine.

SEVEN

IN THE NIGHT I WOKE, not to a nightmare, but the haunted strains of a violin. There were random noises at all hours in this place, but this one was soothing, and I relaxed back into my pillow, not wanting the music to end.

Whatever it was, it was beautiful.

I closed my eyes, and lost myself to sleep.

The morning sun streamed through the window. Relishing my freedom, I hadn't pulled the curtains. Even through the glass, the feel of the sun on my face was indescribable.

True freedom.

I yawned, rolling over to look at the clock. *Shit.* Nearly nine thirty.

Like a zombie, I staggered towards the bathroom, throwing myself under a cool shower to wake up. I'd had the most peaceful sleep in months, but wasn't used to it. The memory of the music made me smile.

Hopefully it's not just a one off.

Out of the shower, I looked at the clock again. It was quarter to ten, I'd wasted fifteen minutes in the water trying to wake up. I dragged on a pair of jeans, and threw on a t-shirt. Grabbing my jacket, I headed out the door, bounding down the stairs and only just missing a girl coming up them. I stopped to apologise.

Holy shit.

She was gorgeous, with long blonde hair in big curls, and deep brown eyes that I found myself falling into. One eyebrow slowly lifted as she took me in, and she smiled shyly, before slowly licking her lips. It was sexy as hell. Didn't hurt that she wore a tank top with no bra underneath, and a short denim skirt. And those legs seemed to go on forever.

"Hi … uh … sorry. I should have been paying more attention to where I was going," I said.

She nodded slowly, her gaze running down my chest before she met my eyes again.

"Yeah, it was a bit my fault too. It's fine." She shrugged. "You must be Andrew. I heard we had a newbie."

I looked at my watch. "Yeah, that's me. Sorry, gotta run. Maybe I'll see you around sometime."

"Maybe." She had that eyebrow raised again as she smiled seductively. Maybe it was my imagination, but she was really interested.

Although, maybe I'd just been away from women too long to read them anymore.

I ran down the rest of the stairs and out to the car. The park wasn't too far to drive to, but I wanted to be there on time. There was no way I wanted to screw up this apology, even if it might be the last time I ever saw Rowan.

Pulling up in the car park, I held onto the steering wheel and closed my eyes for a moment, nervous about seeing her, even more nervous that she wouldn't be there.

Please let her come.

There was half a bag of old bread in the car, part of the groceries that Mum had given me before I left. This would be a perfect distraction from the anxiety that gripped me. There were plenty of ducks, and they'd be grateful for the food.

The weather was chilly with winter on its way, and the park was covered in leaves still falling from the trees shedding their summer coat. This place was beautiful. No matter when you came, there were ducks in the pond. They knew how lucky they were here, being sheltered and fed.

I pulled my jacket tight around me, and ventured towards the pond.

There was a bench not far from the pond and I walked to it, sitting down on the cold wood. Pulling the bag out, I began to throw bread at the ducks. They squawked and flapped their wings in an effort to fight each other for the scraps I threw.

When I ran out of bread, I looked up, just as she sat beside me. Kyle was still, standing and watching as his wife sat to talk to the man who had kidnapped her. I desperately wanted to touch her, just hold her in my arms and embrace the woman who had been my best friend all that time ago, but that would send her running for the hills, and I'd have her husband come down on me with all the force he could muster.

"Hey, Rowan. I'm glad you came to talk to me," I said.

"I'm not here for long, and Kyle is right over there." She shivered. The sky was clouded over, dark and gloomy, threatening to pour with rain.

I shook my head. "I'm not going to try anything. We're way past that. I've had a lot of time to think about what I did, and I can't really believe that I did it."

"I get that you were a bit crazy over Charlie's death. I was devastated too, and you knew it. There's no excuse." She looked at me with those hazel eyes that I still thought about. The fear and outrage that I saw in them for those three days we'd spent together would haunt me forever.

I looked away. "I know, and I'm so sorry. All I could think about was trying to get you to understand that we needed to be together, and yet I knew you were far happier with Kyle than you ever would have been with me. The thought of leaving your baby behind just kills me now. You were so right; I didn't check that Kyle wasn't more badly injured, and just left without another thought. If anything had happened to her ..."

The pain of what happened threatened to engulf me as I spoke. I looked up at Rowan again. Her lips were pressed together like she was suppressing how she really felt. "How is she?" I asked. "How is your little girl?"

Rowan smiled, her pride for her daughter shining for all to see. "She's amazing. Looks a lot like me, straight brown hair. No freckles, though. Well, maybe the odd one, but she's more like Kyle in that way. She's smart and pretty."

"Just like her mother." I had to smile at that; it was always the way I thought of Rowan. Always the smarter one, and despite her not liking the way she looked, she'd always been pretty.

"We've got another one on the way. Early days, but we're hopeful everything will go well." She looked away, towards the ducks that were approaching, looking for more bread. "I wish none of this had happened, Andrew. I could have just pictured yours and Charlie's children playing with mine. We all could have been happy."

I sighed. "I lied about what happened on our honeymoon. Charlie did get upset, but it didn't quite go the way I said. She noticed the way I reacted to Kyle at the wedding, and picked up that I had an issue with him. She loved you so much—she was worried that I might interfere with your relationship, push you further away. That's what we argued about. It was my problem, not yours. I wanted you to know."

Her eyes filled with tears, and she buried her head in her hands. I wanted so much to comfort her, but out of the corner of my eye I saw Kyle running towards us. Any wrong move and he would make sure I was put away again; I knew that. Rowan held up her hand, and he stopped, staring at me as if demanding to know what had happened.

"I loved both of you," she whispered, "but Kyle's all mine. I don't share him with anyone but Mia, and that's different. Maybe I needed for you two to be together in order to find myself. I'm only sorry

Charlie's not here to share this, for me to tell her just how full my life is now. All it took was for me to get over you."

She stood, and my heart broke all over again to look at her. Out of this, I would never be able to salvage any kind of friendship. I would never have her hold my hand, hug me in comfort, pat me on the shoulder to reassure me that despite whatever screw up I'd made, I would still be okay.

The fresh pain I felt at losing her was overwhelming, but I knew I'd suffered that loss three years ago when I'd made my choice and taken her.

"Get better, Andrew. Find a way to move on and be happy. You deserve that." There was nothing in her eyes—no love, no compassion. She was always someone who felt so deeply, and yet now she felt nothing for me.

"Love you, Rowan. Always have, always will," I said.

She turned and walked away before running and leaping into Kyle's arms. He spun her around, and the sound of their shared laughter floated through the air. What I would have given to make her laugh like that.

I watched as he kissed her tenderly. Everything about him screamed of the love he felt for his wife, the one woman I could never have.

I stayed on the bench for a while, watching as they disappeared into the distance. It was over. I'd made my peace with Rowan, but there would be no more *us* in any capacity, and that still tore me apart. So many sleepless nights inside were spent thinking of this moment, when she finally let me go.

Who was I kidding? I let go first when I screwed up.

EIGHT

I DROVE HALFWAY ACROSS TOWN, and back to the boarding house. The sooner I could find a job and get on my feet again, the better. I had to start now.

She stood outside, the girl that I'd seen on the stairs earlier. Her arms were folded defensively as I climbed out the car and walked towards the building.

"Hey," I said.

She uncrossed her arms, reaching for a lock of her hair and curling it around her finger while looking me up and down. It was hot as hell, and my mouth went dry watching this one small act. It had been so long since I'd felt anything for a woman, and this one was pushing my buttons.

"Hey, yourself," she said. She followed me inside, trailing behind me up the stairs.

I turned before going into my unit. "What are you doing?"

"Coming to visit you."

I grinned, shaking my head. "Isn't it polite to wait until you're invited?" I asked.

She swung on her heels, still twirling that lock of hair.

"Look, Whatever-Your-Name-Is, I don't know if you coming to my place is a good idea. How old are you? Seventeen? Eighteen?"

She chewed her bottom lip, reminding me so much of Rowan as she did it. "I'm twenty-two."

"Seriously? You look like you belong in high school. What is your name, anyway?"

She laughed. "Maddy. Short for Madeleine. But if you tell anyone my full name, I know where you live."

I cocked an eyebrow, and wagged my index finger at her. "Sounds like a threat to me. I think I'm going to need to see some proof you're as old as you say you are. Don't want to get into any more trouble with the authorities."

Smiling, she reached out, running her index finger down my chest. "I'll go and find my driver's licence." Leaning over, she whispered in my ear, "And if you're really lucky, I might still have a school uniform buried somewhere in my room."

I shook my head, laughing. "You are going to get me into trouble, aren't you?"

"That's the plan." She bounced away, glancing over her shoulder at the top of the stairs and giving me a look that left me in no doubt that she'd be back.

I rolled my eyes, unlocking the door and pushing it open. I was used to being alone, but after seeing Rowan I felt Charlie's absence more than ever.

We'd been living with Rowan when we'd gotten together. One evening when Rowan was buried in some essay in her room, Charlie and I were studying in the living room, working out something together.

I don't even remember what it was, I'd been so blow away by what had followed, but we'd started arguing about some aspect of what I was writing.

Charlie stood her ground. She was such a quiet, gentle soul, but insanely stubborn. And to be honest, she was probably right, but I wasn't about to let her win.

"You can't come to that conclusion, Andrew. There's so much data you're ignoring."

"No, I've included it. Look further down."

She rolled those big blue eyes of hers, and I grinned at getting that reaction. That was Charlie about to lay down the law, and it always made me laugh. She never got angry. Well, almost never. A stern Charlie was a sight to behold.

"If I read it like this, the tutor will read it like this. Move it so it's nearer the top, and he won't reach this part and think you've missed it."

"Yes, boss," I said, rolling my eyes to follow, and laughing. After all these years, I knew she'd break down if I lightened the mood. She had too much of a sense of humour to ignore it.

Charlie chewed her bottom lip before shoving my shoulder. "Stop it. This isn't funny."

"Of course it is. Nothing's that serious. I'll just cut and paste the paragraph and no one will be any the wiser. Job done."

"But what about—" She never finished the sentence that was bound to point out that moving a paragraph would stop the whole thing making sense. We were so close, she got lost before she found those words, just as I did.

"Charlie," I whispered, reaching for her hand.

Our faces were inches apart, her lips parted, her breathing accelerating as we gazed at one another.

"We can't do this," she whispered.

"Why not?"

"Rowan will never forgive us. She loves you, Andrew."

"I know that. But she's not who I want."

I pressed my lips to Charlie's, ever so gently. When I pulled back, her eyes were closed and she slowly opened them again, showing me her heart.

"Andrew." My name spilled from her lips in a gasp. I'd never heard anything so sexy in all my life.

Before she could protest I kissed her again, and again, never wanting to stop.

Taking her by the hand, I led her to my room, locking the door so we could be alone.

I jumped at the sudden rapping on the door, and opened it to find Maddy waving her driver's licence at me. Maddy Jones.

"Couldn't find the school uniform, but I have this. Will it do?"

I smiled, shaking my head. "You're not going to leave me alone, are you?"

"Hell no. I've waited ages for someone decent looking to move in. You're not getting away."

I roared with laughter, moving aside to let her inside. "Who am I to say no to that?"

Closing the door, I crossed the room to sit on the couch and flicked on the television. Maddy stood in front of me, blocking my vision.

"Do you mind?" I looked up at her.

"I didn't realise I was coming over here to watch television."

I laughed. "It's not like I invited you."

She straddled my lap, rubbing herself against me. "I know; I invited myself. There's no point in holding back now."

My heart pounded, blood rushing in my ears. I should push her off my lap, but I couldn't stop looking at her.

"Maddy," I whispered. She picked up my hand, guiding it under her skirt.

"You're not wearing any underwear," I said.

"No kidding. Get to work, Mister."

I shook my head, pulling my hand away. "As tempting as you are, I can't. I don't just do this."

"Not even for me?"

"We've known each other for what? Five minutes?"

She shrugged. "You kept me waiting while I went to find proof of my age."

I laughed, gently pushing her off my lap. "I'm pretty sure I have a bag of popcorn here if you want to watch a movie with me. That'd be more my pace."

"Spoilsport." She grinned, flopping onto the couch beside me.

"Look, you are gorgeous. There's no doubt about that. But I'm not in any position to start anything, and not irresponsible enough to try anyway."

She sucked in her bottom lip, giving me doubt about the words I'd just come out with. It would be incredibly easy to jump in bed with her, but with Carly giving me a place to live that didn't break the bank, I wasn't about to crap in my own backyard—though Maddy was so damn tempting, I didn't know how long my resolve would last.

Then she shrugged as if she didn't care, and I suppressed a smile.

"There are some DVDs in the box beside the television. Take your pick and I'll throw the bag of popcorn in the microwave."

She shrugged, moving to open the box, screwing up her face at some of the selection. I walked to the cupboard, pulling out the popcorn.

"What sort of movies do you like?" I asked. Apparently my action films were not that impressive.

"Soppy ones. Things that make me cry."

"Do I need a box of tissues for any of those?" I asked, being cheeky while watching the microwave count down.

"Not if this is all you have to choose from." She squealed with delight. "This one."

I looked up. She had a copy of *The Notebook* in her hand. That was one of Charlie's favourites, and her DVD. I'd watched that movie a million times with her, held her while she cried, distracted her by dragging her off to the bedroom to make love after.

"I don't know if I can watch that." I focused on the microwave as it beeped. The popcorn was done, and now I didn't know if I could back out given that I'd let her make the choice.

"Why not?"

"It belonged to my wife. It was a favourite of hers."

"Oh. I can pick something else if you want me to."

I turned back towards her. Those beautiful lips were down-turned. I growled, causing her to look up in surprise. "Fine. We'll watch it. But I choose the next one."

She smiled, and it was like the veneer came off as she let go of that over-the-top persona she'd brought in. "Yay. It's a deal."

I walked back to the couch, sitting beside her, and placing the popcorn between us. Handing her a box of tissues from beside the couch, I shook my index finger at her. "Your tears, your responsibility."

Maddy laughed. "Thank you."

"You know you're much easier to deal with when you're not coming on to me."

At that she cocked an eyebrow.

"It's nice just to have some companionship. It's been a while."

That contented her, and she sat happily watching the movie as I glanced at her. She really was pretty, and I wondered what she'd seen in this place. At least she was safe with me.

Of course the tears began to flow at some point in the film, and I sighed, looking at the ceiling as tissue after tissue scraped through the cardboard opening at the mouth of the box.

"Are you okay?" I asked, looking back at her, already knowing the answer.

"It's ... just ... so ... beautiful," she said between sobs.

"Maybe we should watch something else, take a break from this."

She shook her head wildly, clutching a tissue to her nose. "No. There's not that much left."

"I'm sure there's a Bruce Willis film in there that's much less likely to make you cry."

The sound that came from her was a mix between a sigh and a sob, and she threw herself into my chest face-first.

Here I was, on the couch with a weeping woman I'd only met a couple of hours before in my arms.

I looked back at the ceiling as if to find some kind of divine inspiration in how to handle this, my arms flailing as Maddy's tears soaked my shirt. Nothing came to me.

"Shhh," I said softly.

She looked up at me, her eyes already rimmed with red. "I'm sorry."

This was confusing as hell. Having her so close was definitely having an effect on my body; I was more aroused than I had been in forever. But my heart went out to her; she was such a sensitive soul, just like Charlie had been, to be so upset at a movie.

I sighed. "It's okay." Tentatively, I wrapped my arms around her, closing my eyes and hoping it brought her the comfort she needed before she noticed my hard-on. The last time I'd been with a woman had been some time after I fell out with Rowan. That was a lifetime ago in the scheme of things.

Maddy sat up, and I held my breath, just waiting for some smart remark. She didn't seem the type to miss anything.

"I know it's silly. I watch these things because I know they'll make me cry, and then get pissed off because they make me cry." She laughed, dabbing her nose with the tissue that must have been soaking by now.

"I think I understand," I said.

Sometimes it felt good to cry.

NINE

I STARED AT THE COMPUTER, trying to focus. The words on the screen all merged into a jumble; I must have applied for twenty jobs already, and it was only my fourth day here.

Screw it, that'll do.

Pulling out the cable connected to my mobile, I looked at the end of it. This was going to get costly really fast if I didn't find work, so I'd do whatever I could to find a job soon. I'd made a list of places to door-knock, too—anything to keep my independence.

Behind me, the door handle rattled and I turned to see Maddy walking in.

"Aren't you supposed to knock?" I asked, amused at her cheek.

She shrugged. "I was here last night. What difference does it make?"

"Are you always this forward?"

Maddy walked towards me, stopping as her breasts came in close to my face, her nipples like pebbles at the front of her shirt. *Still no bra.* If I were a lesser man, I would have leaned forward and buried myself in her cleavage. As it was I could smell her perfume, spicy, oriental perhaps. The scent made me feel as if my body were waking from some deep slumber.

"Actually, no. But, I know what I like, and I know Mum wouldn't let you live here if she thought you were trouble. I trust her judgment."

Carly's daughter. Shit. I should have put that together.

"I've just finished applying for some jobs. Want a coffee?" I stood, almost face to face with her, watching as her eyes followed my chest. She didn't move, her body pressed against mine. "Maddy?"

Her mouth fell open and she looked up as if she'd been in a trance. "Sorry. Yeah, sure. That would be great."

"Are you alright?" She was checking me out, just as I'd done to her.

"I'm fine." She shuffled back and moved to the couch, sitting down to watch as I went to get the coffee.

"How do you take it?" I asked.

"White, two sugars." She leaned back on the couch, resting her head on the arm and picking up a magazine from the table beside it.

"Do you usually read these kinds of things?" she asked.

"No. I found them in a box. Mum must have thought I'd get bored."

She put the magazine down. "What have you been doing today?"

"Applying for jobs. You?"

"Working."

She moved as I walked to the couch, sitting up to take the coffee.

"What do you do?" I asked, taking a sip. Her nose wrinkled as she took a deep breath over the coffee. "What's wrong?"

Maddy shook her head. "This stuff is awful. If you're going to drink instant, you need something as decent as you can get."

I rolled my eyes. "I don't even know what it is. Mum packed it."

She sighed. The pity in her eyes nearly made me laugh out loud. "You need help, don't you? Aren't you lucky you have me?"

I should have told her to leave, sent her packing to her own room, but there was just something about her. Besides, I didn't think Maddy was the type of person you could say no to.

"Are you going to take me grocery shopping?" I teased, grinning at her.

She ran her finger around the top of the cup before slowly raising it to her mouth and sucking the coffee off it. This woman knew what she did to me, I was sure of it.

"Okay. Then I can pick out what I want," she said.

Damn cheek. I loved it, laughing and shaking my head.

"Your taste can't be any worse than mine. You're on. But I don't have an endless budget, and I get to pick some things *I* like."

AN HOUR later we were traipsing through the supermarket. I was anyway, following along behind Maddy with the trolley. She'd found the coffee she wanted, and picked out a few things in the confectionary aisle.

I had no idea why I was letting her push me around so much, but I kind of liked it. We did argue in the aisle with the toiletries as she tried to change my deodorant because she liked the smell of something else better.

"I don't mind you choosing new coffee, but I like what I use."

She rolled her eyes. "It's okay, but this one is nicer."

"Maddy, I would rather spend the money on food than things I don't actually need. I already have deodorant"

Maddy's lips turned down into a frown, and she spun away from me.

"I was just trying to help. You'll be going to job interviews and I want you to find something soon."

I let go of the trolley, placing my hands on her shoulders. "I know, and I appreciate that. If you really want me to try it, I will."

She shrugged off my hands, turning to face me. "You don't have to."

"Now you're going to make me feel guilty," I said.

She smiled, looking at me shyly from under her eyelashes. Her eyes were so beautiful, and I was lost for a moment imagining myself grabbing her, kissing her. Holy shit, everything she did was hot.

"Throw it in the trolley before I change my mind."

She grinned, dropping the spray can into the trolley. As she walked past me to go down the rest of the aisle, she stood on her toes, whispering in my ear. "That smell really turns me on. That's why I want you to wear it."

I burst out laughing, and she skipped off leaving me standing there, shaking my head.

We grabbed Chinese takeaway on the way back to the house, and sat watching television and eating Chicken Chow Mein. Apart from the stupid argument at the supermarket, we liked a lot of the same things. I had to admit, she was great to hang out with.

We sat close, Maddy engrossed by whatever was on the television. I have to admit, I didn't care what the show was.

I was too busy looking at her.

TEN

MY EYES WERE REFUSING to open, the drowsiness of sleep stopping me from seeing what had caused the sudden temperature rise in my bed. It had been so warm last night, I'd crawled into bed in just my boxer shorts. Now I felt soft skin against my arm as someone was under the covers with me, and as I roused myself from my slumber, the scent of Maddy's perfume overwhelmed my senses.

Those big, brown, soulful eyes of hers looked out over the top of the blanket.

"What the hell are you doing in my bed, and how did you get in here? You left last night and went back to your own room."

"Hiding. I took the spare key from Mum," Maddy whispered.

"From what?"

"We got a warning from Bob that Dad was on his way. I got out before he arrived and harassed me for money. Mum's probably called the police, but I wanted to be safe."

I sat up, sighing and looked down at her. All I could see was the top of her head down to her eyes—everything else was hidden under the covers. Something about this absurd situation made me laugh, and I gave into it, despite my concern for Carly.

"You think being in my bed makes you safe?" I sat up. If Carly was in trouble, she might need my help.

She nodded, turning her face towards me. "You have really nice abs. Has anyone ever told you that?"

"Is your mother going to be okay?"

The blanket came down just that little bit more and she pouted. "Depends on how drunk he is. I ran, just in case."

I shook my head. "All the way to my bed."

"I know I'm safe here. It's not like *you're* going to try anything." She tilted her head, pursing her lips and raising an eyebrow. "Are you naked under there?"

Her hand slid across the bed, landing on my thigh. I placed my hand on hers, lifting it, amused by her cheek, a little irritated she was making a move when her mother could be in trouble. "No, I'm not naked, and I think I should get out of bed and check on your mother."

She frowned as I threw the covers back, and pulled a shirt on. Her eyes were focused on my boxer shorts, and I reached down, grasping her chin and raising her eyes to my face. "See? I wasn't naked."

Sighing loudly, she threw back the covers and sat up. Still dressed in what I assumed were her pyjamas—boxer shorts and a tank top—she stood, watching as I dragged my jeans on.

"Whose bed did you escape to before I got here?" I asked.

"He's never come over this early. Normally he sleeps off whatever hangover he has before he comes looking for money."

I grabbed her hand. "Come on, let's go sort this out."

Carly's door was shut when we got there, and the place was quiet with no sign of trouble. Bob stood outside, a hang-dog look on his face.

"What's going on?" I asked.

"False alarm. Carly knew. Said it was far too early in the day."

Maddy put her hands on her hips, smiling smugly.

"Wait. So you climbed into my bed knowing nothing was going on?"

The door opened and Carly appeared, coffee cup in hand, smirking at her daughter. "You found a safe haven, then."

Maddy yawned. "Guess I'm going back to bed, then." She turned, walking towards the stairs, presumably back to my bed.

I watched as she made her way up, shaking my head. Whether I wanted it or not, it appeared I had a houseguest.

"She likes you," Carly said, placing her hand on my arm.

"I get that feeling." I laughed. "She's sweet, but very forward." I tried to plead with my eyes, beg Carly to help me understand the whirlwind that was her daughter.

"Andrew, she's not like that with everyone, despite what you might think. She's taken a shine to you. That's good for Maddy." She narrowed her eyes. "I don't know how you feel about it."

I grinned. "To be honest, I don't know how I feel about it."

Carly squeezed my arm. "Don't let her bully you into anything you don't want."

"It's far too late for that," I said, looking up towards my room. Maddy stood at the top of the stairs, and I rolled my eyes, setting off after her.

By the time I got back to my bed, Maddy was already nestled in and I stripped off, climbing into bed with just my boxers on. Still tired, I just wanted to go back to sleep. I didn't know if I could move her if I wanted to.

"Do you snore?" she asked.

"How would I know? I'm usually asleep during the time I might snore."

She laughed, rolling to her side away from me. "I'll let you know if you disturb me."

"I'm sure you will," I said.

I listened to her breathing until it slowed, falling into the rhythm of sleep. My eyes fought me to close, and I gave in, ready to drown in the sleep that beckoned.

Charlie straddled my hips, rocking back and forward, her hair falling over her face. She flicked it back as she gazed into my eyes, and brought me closer to my peak. Her body was beautiful. She was voluptuous, no doubt about that, and I loved every inch, every curve, every touch.

She had full breasts, perky with light pink nipples that were so beautiful against her white, soft skin. I adored her, worshipped her, and then hurt her with my confusion over Rowan.

I'd give anything to have her back again.

I woke to find myself spooning with Maddy, pressed against her body, my nostrils full of her perfume. She smelled so good, and my body had reacted to her as she pressed her backside against me in her sleep.

Her head rested in the nook of my shoulder, and I didn't have the heart to pull my arm away.

"Someone's happy to be with me," she murmured, laughing.

I pulled back. "Sorry."

She rolled over to face me. "You don't have anything to be sorry about. Want me to take care of it?"

"Maddy, I'm not ... "

She growled as she pushed me onto my back, her hand already reaching into my boxers. My mind went blank as she started to stroke me, her soft hands nearly breaking me as I had my first intimate contact with a woman in more than three years.

I'd been about to say that I wasn't after anything. Instead I groaned, about to explode if she kept going.

She slid my boxers down just far enough to expose me, growling again.

"Maddy," I whispered. She ran her tongue over my length before taking as much in her mouth as she could. I moaned, running my fingers through her hair as she began to move up and down. I knew I should stop her, but I couldn't—it felt better than anything had in a long time. She had me under her spell as I watched that gorgeous woman work her magic.

I fought the urge that threatened to overwhelm me as her tongue flicked over, under, all around until I couldn't hold back any longer and let go, hearing her swallow, feeling her tongue slide over me one last time before she joined me back on the pillows.

"Well?" she asked, the smugness radiating from her.

"I might just keep you on," I said, nodding. "Though, before anything else, you need to brush your teeth."

"Is that right?" She cocked an eyebrow, propping herself up on the pillow to look at me.

"Morning breath. Combined with blow job breath, probably not the best." I grinned, and she giggled, moving closer. "After all, you did just give me a blow job without us kissing first. We're not really doing things in the right order."

Maddy leaned over, grazing my lips with hers. "Who says there's a right order?"

I flipped her over onto her back, deepening the kiss, her soft body reacting to mine. It had been so long since I'd had that warmth beside me, and she wanted me, really wanted me.

Her lips parted, her breathing growing heavy as I ran my hand up her thigh, and she pushed at her shorts, dropping them to her ankles, giggling, then pulling me down for another kiss.

"Touch me," she whispered. I didn't need any other invitation, pushing my fingers into her, my thumb grazing her clit. "Andrew."

"Maddy." With my other hand, I pushed up her top to see those breasts, the nipples that had teased me every day with those tank tops she wore. I'd wondered if she owned a bra, she never seemed to wear one. She moaned as I ran my tongue over a nipple, sucking it gently into my mouth.

"I like you like this," I said, my fingers growing wet as she thrust against my hand.

"Like what?" Her breathing was laboured, her eyes heavy as I grew closer to making her come.

"This. No bullshit and bravado. Just you."

"Bullshit and ..." She threw her head back, quivering as her body took her over the top.

"Just you, Maddy. Just you," I whispered. Her nipple had beaded from my attentions, and I went back to licking it, loving it.

"Shit," I said. I put my head on her chest, not wanting to meet her eyes.

"What is it?"

"I don't have any condoms." I looked back up at her with the most innocent look I could muster.

"Oh, you are kidding."

I shook my head. "To be fair, I didn't think that the hot girl I met on the stairs three days ago would end up in my bed. At least not this soon."

She rolled her eyes, sliding out from under me and pulling her shirt down, her pants up. "Fine. I'll go and get some and then we'll see if I'm still in the mood when I get back."

When she was gone, I buried my face in the sheet where she'd been. Her scent was still there, and I closed my eyes, wondering if that was the closest I was going to get to being with her. *What an idiot.*

A few moments passed, and when I heard the door, I sat up, only to be hit in the face with a handful of condoms. Maddy stood beside the bed, pouting. She stripped off her top and pants, climbing back into bed, naked.

"You had better make this worth my while now."

She fixed her gaze on me, those eyes that had so much emotion that belied her attitude.

"Pretty sure I can make it worth it," I murmured, slipping my arm across her. I kissed her, finding her tongue with mine. "You're cold."

"Because you made me get out of bed."

"We could have just not had sex." I pulled her closer, sliding my fingers back into her. "Now, where were we?"

"At the point where you were making this worth it?" She winked, and I laughed, shaking my head.

I spread her legs, moving between them. "You know, if I was a total bitch, I would tell you that my last boyfriend was a god at eating pussy," she muttered.

I took a deep breath, cocking an eyebrow. "Just as well you're not a total bitch then."

It had been so long since I'd gone down on a woman, and I was not about to waste this opportunity. For her, or for me. The way she started thrusting towards me, gasping and raking my scalp? I was pretty sure she wasn't hating it.

"Not ... fair ..." she muttered between breaths, pulling my hair.

I laughed against her skin, kissing her thighs before returning to the scene of my crime. At the risk of sounding cocky, some skills are never lost. This was kind of like riding a bicycle.

After a while of lavishing attention on every part of her I could see, I raised my head. "Want to tell your last boyfriend that he's not the only game in town? And I claim this part."

Maddy laughed. "I'm sorry. I was just pissed at having to stop just to get condoms. Mum didn't even notice me coming and going, she was watching some soap opera."

"I think I can forgive you. Although, I do feel naughty. I'm defiling you while your mother watches television downstairs."

She looked thoughtful. "I like that word. Defiling. Can you do it some more?"

I sat up, picking up a condom packet.

"Why, I would love to defile you, Miss Jones."

She grinned, that devilish grin that I just wanted to kiss off her face.

"Would you like to do the honours?" I handed her the condom, and she laughed as she opened it. Her fingernails were painted a vibrant red and I had this sudden urge to have them scratching down my back.

With one swift move she rolled it on, then lay back and beckoned me forward. She didn't have to ask twice as I moved just as quickly, making her gasp as I took her, driving in deep to claim the rest of her body.

"Come here," I whispered, pulling out and sitting up, beckoning her toward me this time. She straddled me, joining us at the hip, wrapping those gorgeous, long legs around me. If this wasn't heaven, it was pretty damn close.

Our gaze locked, and something happened. My stomach felt as if there were butterflies battling to get out as the spontaneous sex turned into more. I didn't want to ever come. I wanted her to stay hooked around me, needing the contact with her.

She raised a hand, touching her palm to the side of my face as we moved together. A simple gesture, but I wanted as much skin on skin as I could get.

Maddy was beautiful, perfect—*mine*.

She leaned back so I could kiss her breasts, and I ran my lips over them, touching as much of her as I could. I couldn't get enough.

"Are you always like this?" she asked, grinning like the damn Cheshire cat. Every little thing she did just drove me further and further into the madness that was screwing someone I'd only just met.

"It's been a while. I'm making the most of it while it lasts." I kissed her, finding her tongue with mine, my senses in overload. Feeling her, smelling her, tasting her—I couldn't hold on any longer, pulling her hard and rough against me as I let go.

"Keep doing that and it'll last, I think I could do this a lot" she said, giggling as I collapsed onto her, resting my arms on her shoulders.

"You're naughty, Miss Jones," I said, grazing her lips with my own.

"If I am, so are you," she said.

We gently untangled our limbs, and I left her lying in bed while I disposed of the condom. Whatever had happened, whatever this was, it felt more right than anything had in forever.

I slid back into bed, turning to face her.

"So, what is this?" I asked, running my fingers through the

tangled blonde curls falling over my face as she wriggled back to spoon.

She shrugged. "I don't know. Friends with benefits?"

"I don't know if we've known each other long enough to be friends yet."

Maddy rolled over wearing a grin so big it lit the room. "I guess we just skipped to the benefits part. Now we can work on the friends bit."

For probably the first time in my life, I had absolutely no idea what to say.

ELEVEN

MADDY LAY in bed next to me, her hair tousled from all the rolling around we'd done. She looked so sweet as she slept, and I closed my eyes to listen to her breathing, slow and steady.

Rowan had been away for the weekend, visiting her parents, so Charlie and I went crazy, making up for the secrecy we normally surrounded our relationship in.

We had sex in every room in the place, except for Rowan's. When we were finished, we collapsed on my bed, sweaty and panting, Charlie's hair all over the place.

"Damn you're sexy," I whispered, tugging a lock of her hair gently.

"I don't feel it. I just want to sleep now."

I shook my head. "No stamina. That's your problem."

She rolled her eyes at me. "Whatever. Let's get some sleep. We'll have to tidy up tomorrow. Rowan will be back."

Now we were lying face to face, and I kissed her gently. "Let's tell her," I said.

Charlie sighed. "We can't. You know we can't."

"She's got to find out sometime."

"I know." She pouted. "We will tell her, just not yet."

And those big blue eyes sucked me in again as she snuggled up close to me. I would have done anything she told me to.

"Ready to go?" Maddy's voice broke through my daydream, and I turned to see her watching me.

"You were asleep a second ago."

She ran her finger down my chest. "Call it a power nap. Now I'm refreshed."

I groaned, shaking my head. "Do you ever stop?"

Maddy laughed. "Never."

"WHAT HAPPENED TO YOUR WIFE?" It's such an innocent question. Maddy had no idea what she was prying open with it.

"Why do you ask?"

"That DVD the other day. You said it belonged to your wife. You referred to her in the past tense. Did you get divorced?"

I raised an eyebrow. "How I ended up inside. It all leads back to her."

Her eyes widened, and her mouth hung open, but she still clung to me. "Did you kill her?"

"Oh dear God, Maddy, no. She died, but it was an asthma attack. I tried to get her to the hospital in time ..." I stopped, unable to continue that sentence, the thought of Charlie in my arms still so fresh after all this time.

Maddy's eyes filled with tears. "I'm so sorry," she whispered. "What happened after that?"

I couldn't speak for a moment, opening and closing my mouth a couple of times. Trying to find the words to explain to her what I'd done.

She kissed my chest softly, warm tears dropping onto my skin and rolling down my side. "Sorry," she whispered.

"Don't be sorry. If we're going to keep doing this whatever we're doing, I need to tell you." I sucked in a deep breath, closing my eyes to centre myself before opening them again. "I felt so lost without Charlie, so I tried to turn to my old friend Rowan. She'd had a crush on me for years and I got it into my head that Charlie would want me to move on with her."

Maddy looked up at me, her eyes full of sorrow.

"I became so obsessed with it all. Rowan was in love with someone else, she married him, had a baby with him, and I still couldn't see past my own nose. Her husband told me to leave her alone and I flipped, kidnapped her and held her captive for three days until we got found. That's what I went to prison for."

I closed my eyes as Maddy stroked my cheek. "That must have been awful for you and her," she said softly.

"I lost my two best friends. I got so lost. A lot of it is a blur. I remember being desperate for Rowan to see things my way, and I couldn't see anything else. When the police found us, it was as if I woke up and came back to reality."

Opening my eyes, all I could see now was Maddy. "I was broken. I can't say I'm over it all now, but I'm a long way from where I was three years ago." I stroked her hair, feeling her gentle kisses on my chest. "You wouldn't have wanted to know me then, but all of this made me grow up."

She looked up at me again, that cheeky grin of hers lighting up her face. "I'm glad one of us is."

I laughed, squeezing her tight, breathing in that heady spicy fragrance. On anyone else it would have driven me mad; on Maddy, it was intoxicating.

Three days, and I was crazy about this girl. Blindsided by her attentions, I was happier than I felt I had any right to be. The mixed emotions swirled around, the combination of excitement over starting something new and guilt for needing to move on.

"She would understand," Maddy whispered the words I needed to hear as if on cue.

"Are you going to let me sleep tonight? I think I need to get some rest before going job hunting tomorrow," I said, trying to change the subject.

Maddy winked at me. "I think I can let you get a few hours. Don't be surprised if you wake up to me helping myself."

If nothing else, she made me laugh, made me feel good about myself. Which was more than I had in longer than I could remember. I could very easily fall in love with her.

TWELVE

THREE DAYS.

That was how long Charlie and I were married before she died in my arms. If I could turn back the clock and get her back, I would in a heartbeat. I'd always love her; never take her for granted. Without that as an option, I needed to move on with my life, somehow find happiness again.

Three Days.

Rowan had loved me her whole life and I knew it. I saw the puppy eyes, and the sulky looks whenever I got a girlfriend. She was one of my best friends, and I adored her. And I kept my biggest secret from her. When I lost the plot, I held her captive for three days, trying to convince her that she should be with me. As if that could ever make up for the loss of Charlie.

Three Days.

Maddy snorted and rolled over. I couldn't help but smile at the sight of her sleeping peacefully, right where she wanted to be. Right where I wanted her to be. We met three days ago, and she'd already found her way into my bed. This should be too much, too fast, but it just felt good. Just to have her beside me in bed brought comfort.

I lay on my back and stared at the ceiling. This emotional shit was so hard to get my head around. How fast was this going to progress if it was more than just friends with benefits? Was I over-thinking it?

Rolling over to watch Maddy sleep again, I wanted to hold her tight, lose myself in her again. We'd been in bed for I don't know how many hours now, alternating between making love and sleeping, and I didn't know if I wanted to get out again.

A SCREECH near my ear brought me back to life with a jolt. I must have fallen asleep again, and now Maddy was waking with a roar as she sat up in bed, clinging to the sheets, fear in her eyes.

"Maddy?" I murmured, still sleepy.

"Sorry," she whispered, lying back down and pulling the blanket up again. "I had a nightmare."

I opened my arms and she rolled into them, snuggling up tight.

"You okay?" I whispered, nuzzling her ear.

"I dreamed of Dad. Last time he was here, the cops took ages to come and he hit Mum so many times."

"Baby." I stroked her cheek with my hand, feeling so protective, so angry on her behalf.

"She was so bruised. I'm so scared he'll come one day and kill her, or me."

I tilted her face towards me with my fingers. Her eyes told me she believed what she was saying.

"I'll do whatever I can to protect you—I hope you know that. This whatever-it-is we've started feels so good, and your mother has been great letting me stay here. I'm not about to let either of those things go in a hurry."

She smiled, lifting her hand to my face and running her thumb across my lips. "You're a good man, Andrew Carmichael. Don't let anyone tell you otherwise."

"You don't even know me."

"You didn't kick me out of bed when you found me here, and you didn't make a move on me. Therefore, you're okay."

I cocked an eyebrow. "Right."

Her face lit up with that amazing smile, and I kissed her tenderly. "I have nightmares too," I whispered.

"What about?"

"Rowan mostly. A lot of what I did is a blur, but in my dreams, I remember her screaming at me to let her go home." I felt the tears building, and fought them. While I thought I was telling Maddy this to bring her some comfort that she wasn't alone in her dreams, it just brought all those feelings I had when I woke to the surface.

"Andrew," she whispered, her gentle touch to my face bringing me the comfort I sought to give her.

"I did such an awful thing, Maddy. You should run as far away from me as you can."

Maddy smiled, her fingers resting on my cheek. "I'm far from perfect. You're not the only one who's been in trouble with the law."

"Really?"

"I acted out when things were bad at home. I shoplifted, and got caught. I was probably doing it to get attention for what was happening for Mum. The cops brought me home and they saw her, realised something was going on."

I sifted her hair through my fingers, listening to her speak. She'd clearly been through so much. Maybe we weren't that different.

"That's when I got this." She turned her back to me, and I spotted the faint line running down her back, where the skin was just a little lighter than the rest.

"What is it?" The puckered flesh beneath my finger was tough to the touch in contrast to her smooth, soft skin. What had been done to her to create a scar like this lit a fire in my belly.

"When the police left, Dad hit me with his belt, really hard. That was when Mum had enough. She'd put up with him doing it to her, but as soon as he laid a hand on me …"

She rolled back towards me. Our faces were inches apart, and there was more than just the lust I'd seen earlier in her eyes. Neither of us could speak, our eyes locked together in some shared empathy for one another. We'd both had pain in our lives; now we'd shared our pasts.

But what about the future?

And why on earth was I thinking that after only knowing her three days?

Almost as if she could read my mind, she licked her lips, her eyes darkening as her hand roamed down my chest.

"I don't know what this thing we've started is, or why I wanted it so bad. Something about you called to me," she whispered.

I closed my eyes as her hand worked its magic, her fingers like silk against my skin, calling my body to life to give her what we both needed.

It was too soon, too fast, and I had no intention of changing a thing.

THIRTEEN

THREE WEEKS.

Maddy and I had been involved for three weeks now, and we were in the that stage where even the thought of her made my stomach flutter like a million butterflies were trying to get loose.

Equally causing me butterflies was the struggle to find a job. It had taken three weeks to secure an interview. The relief at getting to the interview stage was overwhelming, and I'd spent last night working out what to wear.

Maddy had stood over my shoulder, inspecting my choices and telling me what went with what. It had been unnerving; Charlie had once done the same thing. As with Maddy, I'd stood, bemused while she went through my things and found a matching shirt and tie to go with my suit.

I'd bitten my tongue when I'd realised they had very different tastes. Where Charlie had gone for subtle pastel hues, Maddy had managed to dig out the tie I'd worn once, throwing it in a drawer to forget about it forever more. It was a brilliant blue, not my usual style, and I didn't know what had possessed me when I'd bought it.

"This makes you look confident about yourself. You're not afraid to be bold."

Now, Maddy gave me strength when I needed it, and I fell deeper as I watched her tying the Windsor knot. She was adorable, her tongue sticking out between her teeth as she put all her concentration into getting the knot right.

I didn't have the heart to tell her I could do it in my sleep.

"There you go," she said. "Go get 'em tiger."

I grinned, pulling her into my arms and planting a kiss on the lips I loved to feel against mine.

"Thanks, Maddy."

She looked at her watch, her eyes widening as she realised the time.

"Crap, I'll be late for work. I've got to go. Good luck."

Maddy kissed me on the cheek, and I let her go, waving her goodbye as she made it out the door. She was really something else.

I made the bed, and washed the breakfast dishes before going downstairs to the car. My interview was at nine thirty and I made the short trip in ten minutes, leaving fifteen more minutes before I was due.

My stomach nearly ate itself with nerves as the clock ticked down to nine twenty and I took a deep breath, making my way to the reception desk.

The first thing I got was the application form to fill in while I waited. It started off simple—name, address, previous experience ... Then on the flip side was the question that stopped me in my tracks—the one I expected, but it still stabbed me in the chest to have to answer.

Do you have any criminal convictions?

I paused, my pen held over the paper, and took a deep breath. Closing my eyes, I took another breath before opening them and writing one word. *Yes.*

I'd known to expect the question, but it still caught me, throwing me off my game.

If I didn't face this now, I'd never get the courage to. I swallowed down my pride, returning the form to the reception desk. The receptionist took it from me with a smile, glancing at the front and flipping it over to make sure I'd filled it in correctly. I waited for some sign that she'd noticed, some indication that I was the scum of the earth.

Instead she nodded, smiling again and asking me to take a seat.

A few minutes later, a woman appeared, her brunette hair swept up off her face in a bun, wearing a tailored suit that clung to her curves. I had a sudden pang of not knowing it I was dressed formally enough. Did I want to work in a corporate-type office? I hadn't even thought about that.

In prison, I'd been able to wear my own jeans and T-shirts. I'd had to dig out my suit from the clothing that had been in storage. I didn't know if I wanted to wear one every day. But then, I couldn't afford to be that fussy.

"Andrew Carmichael? I'm Patricia Morris."

I rose, smiling at her as she extended her hand.

"Come with me. I'll just take you through here and we can have a chat."

I swallowed hard, gathering the courage to follow. She led me through to a room with a large table in the middle and motioned for me to sit.

"Your CV looks good, but I noticed you haven't been working for some time. Maybe we can start with you telling me what you've been doing."

My mouth went dry, and I paused to catch my breath. She looked at me, head cocked, waiting for my answer.

"Actually, I've been in prison."

The awkward silence that followed was made worse by the way she looked at me. Her nose twitched as she processed what I'd said, and her eyes glazed over.

"Oh. May I ask ..."

"It's a really long story, but kidnapping."

She looked down at the table, the application form I filled in shaking as her hands trembled.

"Andrew, I'm sorry ..."

"If you want the whole story, I'm happy to tell you. It's not as dry-cut as it seems. I'm ready to get back to work, and when I do I'll work hard."

Patricia's shoulders slumped, and she frowned as she met my eyes again.

Holy shit. I can't get past the first question.

To her credit, she recovered, smiling slightly and picking up my CV. She started talking about my previous experience, and I answered every question she fired at me. There was no doubt in my mind that I made her nervous, and I couldn't blame her for that.

As I left, I shook her hand again and she nodded. "We'll let you know soon," she said.

"Thank you. I appreciate it."

I walked away, the conflict in my stomach still not resolved. If that was how every interview started, how on earth would I ever find work?

"ANDREW? ANDREW CARMICHAEL." I looked up from the vegetables I'd been inspecting. I'd promised to cook Maddy dinner, and in an attempt to impress her, decided it had to all be fresh and not the frozen foods my meals had consisted of so far.

We'd spent every available moment together, eating noodles and out of cans rather than going anywhere. My days were spent looking for a job, my nights were spent with Maddy. I had applied for welfare, which would cover me for a while longer. As much as I didn't want to go back home to Mum and Dad's, I knew the day could come when I needed to.

Maddy worked in a clothing store, which had come in handy as I updated my wardrobe. Looking good was important. I had to make the best impression I could before breaking the news about what I'd done to potential employers.

A vaguely familiar face came into focus, and I realised I was looking at a woman I'd gone to university with. If only I could remember her name …

"It's Kim, Kim Collins. We were at uni together."

I nodded. "I remember."

"I didn't realise you were out … I mean …" She went scarlet. This was going to be a reaction that I would have to get used to as I ran into people from my past.

"Yeah. About a month ago."

She recovered, tapping my arm. "You're looking good. I was so sorry to hear what happened with your wife and everything. That'd be enough to screw anyone up." Her jaw dropped, and she covered her hand with her mouth, glowing red with embarrassment. "I'm sorry, I didn't mean anything … Go on, Kim, put your foot in it."

"It's okay. I know it's a lot to take in," I said, laughing.

"So, how are you? That's probably a stupid question, given you've had about five minutes to sort out your life." She swung on her heels. *Oh God. Is she flirting with me?*

"Actually, not too bad. Just need to find a job and I'll be on track. How about you?"

She nodded. "Pretty good. We're looking for another business analyst at work. Might be right up your alley, if you're interested. I seem to remember that was what you were doing when things went off the rails."

How much else did she remember about me? Seemed a bit random after all this time.

"Uh, yeah. I'd definitely be interested. In the job, that is."

She grinned, licking her lips. She was gorgeous, but Maddy was already so far under my skin that the action didn't have the effect it might have once upon a time.

"Great. How about we swap numbers and I'll talk to my boss? I can give you a call and let you know if he wants to see you."

"Uh sounds good. I'd appreciate the referral." I pulled out my phone, tapping her number into my address book while giving her my own.

"Yeah well, I never picked you for being that crazy. That whole losing-your-wife-on-your-honeymoon has to be the hardest thing ever." She clapped her hand over her mouth again. "I didn't mean that to come out that way, I was trying to be sympathetic."

"I know. It's okay." It would never be okay, but it was something I had to get used to.

"Anyway, I guess I should leave you to it. Shopping for dinner?"

"Yeah, something like that. I'm cooking for ... for ..." Hell, what was she? "For a friend."

"Oh. Right. Well, have fun. I'll call you." She smiled.

I watched as she walked away. Hopefully something would come of that—at least she would tell her boss I was a kidnapper, that I had a criminal record, and then we could go from there.

The insanity of that thought nearly made me laugh out loud. I stopped myself, though; there were already enough people in the world who thought I was crazy, let alone the other shoppers in the supermarket.

"THIS IS PRETTY AMAZING," Maddy said between mouthfuls. She waggled her eyebrows at me, and I laughed, shaking my head.

"It's really just meat and vegetables."

"Oh, but so perfectly cooked." She slid a piece of carrot between her teeth, and if my temperature didn't shoot up, it gave it a good go. A warm glow washed over me from my head to my feet. Just watching her eat, remembering our recent marathon bed session.

I closed my eyes, shaking it off. "Got a possible lead on a job too. I ran into someone I used to go to uni with, and the company she works for is looking for people."

Maddy cocked her head as I opened my eyes again. "She?"

I laughed. "Trust you to pick that one part of the sentence out."

She grinned, that cheeky grin that got me into trouble in the first place. "I hope it works out. Then you'll be able to keep me in the manner I've become accustomed to."

"What are you talking about?"

Maddy pointed at the meal. "This. I'd like cooking like this every night, thank you."

"So, you only want me for my cooking?"

She leaned over, giving me a view down her top, her hand on my thigh. *This is so hot.*

"No. I want you for much more than your cooking. It's just a great bonus."

I pressed my lips against hers for a quick kiss before standing with my plate, needing to get some space between us. Maddy was charming and funny, and made me hotter than I had been in forever. But, I wanted more. Not just sex, but her friendship.

Even if we joked about being friends with benefits, I wanted the friends part, the emotional attachment. Despite the fact that we were probably going to have sex again tonight, I wanted quality time.

I ran the water in the sink, letting the heat distract me from my torrid thoughts. It'd be easy to just drag Maddy off to bed—I doubted she needed much persuasion—but I'd enjoyed the whole cooking-a-meal-for-someone again, someone who wanted to be with me.

Her scent hit me before her arms wrapped around my waist. "What are you thinking about?" she asked, leaning her head on my back.

"Us."

"So, do you think there is an *us*?"

I turned, picking up a towel from the counter, wiping my hands. "Maybe there could be, if you wanted there to be. I want us to spend time together."

"That's what we are doing, silly."

"I mean, just time hanging out. Not in bed, not having sex—just being together."

Maddy backed away, grabbing my hands and pulling me away from the sink. "Let's snuggle on the couch and talk then."

"You don't mind us not having sex tonight?" I grinned as she backed up against the couch, pulling me towards her.

"I didn't say no sex, but we could spend some time just talking." She looked up at me, so sweet and innocent and for a moment, time stopped as we gazed at each other. I swear I saw her soul. Maddy was so much more than she ever let anyone know.

She'd spent her entire life in this big, old place, keeping things together when everything around her was falling apart. Maybe the house stayed intact for her. Lord knows it should have been down around their ears some time ago.

FOURTEEN

I'D HOPED for a repeat the following night, her companionship comforting, and her presence alluring. I shouldn't have let myself get distracted, but I couldn't help it. I loved everything we did together and couldn't wait for her to touch me again, wanted to know her better.

By the time I got up she'd left for work. She'd spent another night in my bed, but I'd slept so well, I hadn't noticed her slipping out of my arms to leave. The bed was cold, and I clutched her pillow to me, grinning at her scent still faintly there.

I spent the day searching the net for jobs again, applying for a couple more, before surrendering to the couch. I could go out, but that would just waste gas, and I needed to save what I could.

The day dragged, and when Maddy didn't turn up after her shift, I went downstairs to look for her. She was on her way out Carly's door as I got to the bottom of the stairs.

"I've been waiting for you," I said, grabbing hold of her hand.

"Sorry, Andrew. I've got to go." There was no humour in her words, no smile on her face.

"Is everything okay?"

"Fine. I'm out for the evening, might be out for the night. Got some stuff to take care of."

She kissed me on the cheek, pulling her hand away, and walked out the door. I stood like a chump watching her go, wondering what on earth was going on and where she could be going all night.

Who was I kidding? She had her own life to lead, even if part of it was entwined with mine now. I wanted an explanation, but did she owe me one? The confusion tore at my gut, and I climbed the stairs and went back to the television.

When my phone buzzed. I picked it up to a text from Kim.

> Kim: My boss wants to meet you. 10am tomorrow if you're free.

A tiny glimpse of hope began to grow. If I could get the employment part of my life sorted, maybe the rest would fall into place. I had another interview booked for the afternoon; morning should be no problem.

> Me: That would be fantastic.

She sent the address, and I tried to keep focused. Maybe this one would be different. If Kim had told them about me and they still wanted an interview that was one less barrier I'd have to worry about. My mind kept wandering to Maddy.

I hope you're okay.

I WAS out for most of the following day. At least I was prepared for rejection. But, the day didn't go too badly, and I went home to wait for a call about either of them.

Trying to save money, I'd caught the bus. Gas was best left for when I needed it; it was expensive enough. It meant for a much longer day, and by the time I trudged back to the boarding house, I'd already decided to take the car next time. Screw it.

Outside the house and down the road a little was a car. I wouldn't have noticed it, but for Maddy, her arms around the man standing beside it, his hands on the small of her back. They didn't even notice as I drew closer, but my stomach plummeted at the sight of them.

He was tall, with dark hair and stubble. Black jeans and a leather jacket. About the opposite of me. She let go of his neck, and looked at him with the same intensity she used when she looked at me. I couldn't watch.

I ducked into the entrance of the house, not wanting to see any more. What the hell? She'd thrown herself at me, and I had fallen for it hook, line and sinker. Was she warming his bed too?

Barely noticing Bob standing at the base of the stairs, I walked straight into him.

"Shit, man. Sorry," I said. "Distracted."

He grinned. "Is her name Maddy?"

Ugh. This was one conversation I did *not* want to have.

"It's just been a long day. Went to a couple of job interviews today, hoping one will pan out."

He nodded. "It's a tough one. Good luck."

I ran up the stairs and into my room, closing the door behind me and leaning on it. It shouldn't hurt as much as it did. I barely knew her, but she'd opened up to me, told me some of her deepest, darkest fears as I had done with her. My phone buzzed and I pulled it from my pocket.

> Kim: How did the interview go?

> Me: Okay I guess. I'm not getting my hopes up about anything.

Ever.

> Kim: Want to go out for a drink tonight?

My finger hovered over the phone. She was attractive, but the connection wasn't there. Not like it was with Maddy. I closed my eyes, and saw Maddy in the arms of someone else. There was some intimate connection between her and the guy by the car. The way his hands rested on her easily, the way she was snuggled into his neck. The same way she'd snuggled into my neck.

We hadn't made any promises, no commitment to one another. Whatever we had was so new, but we'd been intimate. I'd never been one for just jumping into bed with a woman. I had to feel a connection, like the one I'd felt with Maddy.

> Me: Sounds great. I'll shower and meet you if you text me where you are.

The hot water felt good, cleansing in more ways than one. If that was what Maddy wanted, fine. She could have him. At least I'd seen it with my own eyes, not found out later. Jealousy burned, but I had to extinguish the feeling.

I just hadn't thought it would hurt this much.

After dressing, I went down the stairs, heading out the door to the car. Maddy was coming in the building as I approached the exit.

Hey, how was your day?" she asked cheerily.

"Fine. Sorry, gotta run."

She reached for me as I went past, but I kept going.

"Where are you off to?"

I turned back toward her. "I've got a date. Don't wait up."

It was stupid, hurtful, and I cursed myself as I got in the car. I didn't even stop to see what her reaction was, and I didn't have the guts to go back to check.

Kim sat at the bar, smiling as I approached.

"You made it."

I nodded, leaning on the bar to get a drink and gulping it down as fast as I could.

"Wow. Someone's had a bad day." Her hand landed on my arm, gently squeezing it.

All I could think of was Maddy.

"Another one, please," I said to the bartender. This one went down slower, but after not drinking for so long, I could already feel the effects, becoming warmer in my own skin, relaxing, despite still being stressed about it all.

"Andrew, are you okay?" Kim laughed, tossing her hair and smiling at me in that way.

Holy shit. What am I doing?

"I'll be better when I've wiped today from my mind."

Worry crossed her face, a small dent appearing between her eyebrows as she frowned. "Was the interview that bad?"

"Not the interview. Just stuff."

A sly smile crossed her lips, and she ran her index finger down my chest. "Anything I can distract you from?"

"We'll just have to see what happens, won't we?"

I was giving her false hope; I knew that the moment I opened my mouth. But if I could just pretend to be interested in anyone other than Maddy, maybe I could get through this.

Maddy.

FIFTEEN

THE CRISP NIGHT air filled my lungs, the cold making me cough. My head spun from the amount that I'd drunk.

"Come back to my place," Kim slurred, no better than I was.

I shook my head. "I have to go home. I've got things to take care of."

She pouted. "Are you sure?"

I nodded, waving down a taxi as it dropped someone outside the pub. The driver stopped, and waved back to indicate he was free.

"You can get that taxi, I'll wait for the next one," I said.

Kim grabbed me, pulling my body against hers, her lips pressed against mine as she tried to push her tongue into my mouth. I didn't let her, but I didn't fight her off.

"Maybe another time," she whispered, kissing my cheek.

"I'm seeing someone else."

Even drunk, she processed the words, and backed off, her face stony and cold.

"I'm sorry, Kim. This whole thing. I came out because I think the girl I started seeing is screwing someone else and I ran instead of talking. But all I can think about is her and how much I miss her."

"Here we go again. I'm always the girl who wants the guy who's in love with someone else. Fuck my life." She turned on her heel, storming to the taxi, not looking behind her as she drove off.

I didn't have the energy to protest, to apologise. I just wanted to get home and find out what was going on with Maddy.

Staggering in the front door, I headed straight for Carly's room. I got as far as raising my fist to knock before realising it was twenty-seven minutes past three in the morning. I was drunk, and about as appealing as a drowned rat.

Stumbling up to my room, I flopped face down on the bed. I'd tidy up and go and see her in the morning.

It's already morning.

At some point I rolled over and looked at the clock. It read three forty-five and I knew it was afternoon because it hurt to open my eyes in the bright sunlight streaming through the window.

My stomach grumbled, but my head still spun. I lay back on the pillow and went back to sleep.

IT WAS lunchtime before I woke again, my stomach grumbling, complaining at the lack of food I'd given it during the last couple of days.

I rolled out of bed, grabbing a box of crackers from the cupboard. I sat on the couch, flicking on the television and stuffing my face. This had to make me feel better.

Before climbing on the bed, I hadn't removed any clothing, and I grimaced at the sweaty smell and gross feel of wearing the same clothes for a day and a half.

Food, shower and a coffee. That was what I really needed. And Maddy, to go and work out what was going on with Maddy.

I pressed my palms to my face, groaning at my own stupidity. Instead of lashing out at her, I should have stopped just for a moment and found out what was going on. At least if she was seeing someone else and didn't want to see me anymore, I would have known for sure.

I got as far as lying back on the couch, resting my head on the arm. All that sleep and I was still tired, in need of motivation.

It didn't take long to fall into that half-asleep, hazy state again. Lying on the couch wasn't helpful in that respect.

I jumped at the loud knock on the door, rolling and landing on the floor on my butt. "Who on earth is that?" I grumbled.

Oh shit, it could be Maddy.

Standing, I straightened my tie, brushing my jacket down with my hands. I might be a mess, but I'd be a respectable mess if I could get away with it. Rubbing my chin, I noted the now two-day-old stubble. I must look like crap.

Carly stood there, casting a glance over me and shaking her head. "What on earth have you been doing, Andrew? You look like something the cat dragged in, and I know you were up here all day yesterday."

"I've been sleeping."

"What did you do to Maddy?"

I sighed, shaking my head. Carly fumed at me, tapping her foot on the wooden floor, my head pounding as the sound bore through my brain.

"I saw her with another guy. Look, Carly, I don't know what the story is, but when I was presentable, I was planning on coming down to talk to her and work this out if we can."

She set her jaw. "That other guy was Logan. He's Maddy's ex-boyfriend and still her close friend. They're more like brother and sister now. You're the one she's crazy about."

"She brushed me off to go somewhere for the night and then I see her all tangled up with him. What was I supposed to think?" I was exasperated. Yeah, I'd not stopped to talk to Maddy, but she hadn't told me what she was doing either.

She sighed this time. "Maddy doesn't think things through sometimes. If she didn't tell you where she was going, I understand that it looked bad. I'm sorry, Andrew, but she's been crying for nearly two days now, and I'm worried about her."

My stomach plummeted, and not because of the hangover.

"You smell like a brewery. Let's get you cleaned up so you can go and see her."

Carly pushed past me, heading for the kitchen and grabbed the coffee jar. "You, go and have a shower. Put some clean clothes on."

"Yes, Mum," I said.

She looked up at me, shaking her head, clamping her lips together as she tried her best to hide her amusement.

I grabbed a clean T-shirt and jeans, and disappeared to have the hottest shower I think I've ever had. I was pretty sure Carly was out there running water to push the temperature up.

It turned out to be what I needed. My skin tingled from the heat of the water, and the soap soon got rid of that awful lying-in-bed sick sensation.

After brushing my teeth twice, I headed back out to Carly. She smiled, handing me a coffee. "Much better."

"Carly, I'm sorry."

"Save it for Maddy. She's the one who's hurting."

The sound of sniffing came over the top of the blanket as I entered the room. She faced away, and I think she just assumed I was her mother, as she didn't move when I sat on the bed.

I'd never been in there. There was a music stand in the corner, a guitar against the wall, and on the small desk at the end of the bed was a violin. The source of my mystery music.

"I hear you've been crying for two days," I said, placing my hand on her arm.

Maddy rolled over, pushing my hand away. Heavy, red-rimmed eyes were all I could see, that soft skin of hers bloated from the tears.

"No. I got something in my eye." Always defiant, never giving in.

"Both of them? For two days?"

She sniffed loudly. "Yeah. It took something big to do this much damage. Pretty sure it was your ego."

I couldn't help the smile that spread across my face. "Ouch." Raising my hand to her cheek, I wiped the new tear that rolled down. "Lucky you have that much liquid in your body. I didn't come in here and find a shrivelled up prune."

She bit her bottom lip, suppressing the laughter that threatened to make its way out. "You're a jerk. You know that, right?"

"Yes. I am a jerk. But, if I promise not to be so stupid again, will you forgive me? I got everything wrong, and I should have talked to you. Not been a bigger jerk."

"I didn't do anything bad." She sniffed, her breaths growing shorter as the tears threatened again.

"I know you didn't. If it makes you feel better, I didn't enjoy myself. Even when she kissed me goodnight, all I thought about was you."

Maddy sat up, her face darkened with anger. "Wait. You kissed her?"

Shit.

"Well, kind of. She kissed me. It was the end of the night, and we were saying goodbye and she kissed me."

Her voice rose, and I prayed Carly wouldn't hear. "What? I did nothing, Andrew. Nothing. And here you are, making out with someone else five minutes after sleeping with me. Screw you."

She turned her back on me again, lying down and hugging her pillow tight to her. I could have walked away, moved out, pretended none of this had ever happened, but Maddy was the first, the only one I'd wanted in so long.

"Maddy," I whispered, lying on the bed beside her and snuggling up to her back. "I'm sorry. I'm so, so sorry. I saw you with that guy and it drove me crazy. You two looked so intimate and I was jealous."

"Logan is like a brother to me," she said between sobs.

"I get that now. I can't tell you how sorry I am. I'll do whatever it takes to make it up to you. If I can. Please."

She rolled over to face me. "I don't know if you can. I don't think I did anything to deserve you doing that."

I stroked her face, pushing her hair back behind her ear. "You didn't. It was entirely my fault. Old habits—rushing into stupid shit that I shouldn't have. I have no idea where this is going, Maddy, but the only person I was thinking of when I went on that damn date was you. I missed you so much."

"I missed you too." Her arms slid around either side of my neck, and we just lay there, clinging to one another.

There was nowhere else I wanted to be. I just hoped like hell she knew it.

"Logan just went through some really bad stuff with an ex, and wanted to talk about it. So, I crashed on the couch at his place and we stayed up until early morning. He just needed a friend."

I kissed her forehead, lingering over her face as I breathed in her scent, grounding myself.

"I guess we both could have communicated better," she whispered. "I didn't even think about it. I'm not used to having someone at home who gives a crap, except for Mum and Bob."

"I'm here, and I give a crap," I said, tenderly kissing her lips, her cheeks, looking into those eyes that had been so sad, but now had a glimmer of a smile.

I had no idea where we were going, but I wouldn't want to be anywhere else.

SIXTEEN

"DON'T you think it's a bit too soon to be involved with someone? You've only been here a month," my mother asked, stroking my arm ever so lightly. They'd arrived ten minutes before and I was already feeling under scrutiny.

"It's nothing serious. At least, not yet. She's fun to be around, and we're enjoying ourselves. Is there anything wrong with that?" I sighed, knowing I needed to downplay it or I'd never hear the end of this.

"I worry, Andrew. After everything that happened, I worry that you might get too attached to her, and if it goes badly—"

"I'll kidnap her and disappear? Is that what you're trying to say, Mum?" I glared at her, stopping her in her tracks before she could try to go there.

I sighed again, leaning back on the couch and looking at the ceiling. "I've changed a lot since I've been away. I thought you, of all people, would recognise that and support me. Seriously." I looked back at my mother. Her brows were furrowed, her eyes full of concern. "Maddy is special. She knows exactly what she's getting with me, and she wants me anyway. If it lasts then it lasts, if it doesn't, we'll both move on. Right now, I can't tell you which way it's going to go because it's new, and it's pretty damn wonderful after feeling nothing for so long."

Dad's hand landed on my knee. "It's okay, Andrew. Mum worries; that's all. I do too, but I know we need to give you the space you need to work these things out. Hell, if I could convince you to come home with us, I'd get you out of here in a heartbeat."

I placed my hand on top of Dad's, squeezing it to thank him. "There's more chance of me finding work here, and my counsellor is here. Nowhere else makes sense for me to be. Besides, I can't stay where Charlie is. I can't get bogged down with all those memories. I have the welfare payments. I know I can't live on it forever, but it's enough right now."

Mum stood, going back to the counter in silence to make more coffee.

"She understands, Son, she really does. It's a lot of take in. You're back and then you're gone again."

There was a knock on the door, and I got up to answer, laughing as I saw who was on the other side, and what she was wearing. "Why are you knocking?" I stifled a laugh, and got a pinch to the stomach in response.

"I'm being polite," said Maddy through gritted teeth. A white, collared blouse and long black skirt made her look like some kind of old-fashioned school ma'am.

"Mum, Dad, this is Madeleine," I said, smiling sweetly. Maddy scowled at me before breaking out into a big, welcoming smile for my parents.

CARLY WAITED at the bottom of the stairs, greeting us as we descended. I smirked at Maddy's face. Her mother was wearing her trademark jeans and Metallica shirt. Not the image Maddy was trying to convey. Maddy frowned and rolled her eyes as we drew closer.

"Mum, Dad, this is Madeleine's mother, Carly."

Maddy glared at me while Carly laughed, reaching out to shake hands with Dad.

"Madeleine?" She looked at Maddy while shaking her head.

I laughed, shaking my head. "Sorry, baby," I murmured, kissing Maddy while my parents introduced themselves to Carly.

"You'll keep," she said.

"That's what I'm counting on." I looked around at the parents engrossed in talking to each other, then slid my hand down her back, squeezing her butt cheeks.

"What are you doing?" she hissed.

"Checking if you're wearing underwear."

She slapped my arm as Dad looked up. "You two ready for dinner?" He smiled at Carly. "Do you want to join us?"

Carly shook her head. "Not this time. I've got a new guest arriving shortly and I like to make sure I greet them myself. Have fun."

"We will," Mum said brightly.

Maddy's eyes were big as saucers as we entered the restaurant. "I've never been anywhere this fancy," she whispered.

The tables were candlelit, with sparkling white crockery and shiny cutlery that glittered in the dusky light.

As we were shown to our table, she marvelled at the waiter pulling out her chair, and gasped at the white cotton napkins, embroidered with the restaurant logo.

Nails latched onto my leg when the menu came out, and I could see the sheer terror in her eyes at ordering the pricey dishes. Dad hadn't cut any corners; he seemed to be out to impress.

It was working. I held her hand under the table to reassure her, and despite her trembling at times, she handled the situation without skipping a beat. She was better at pronouncing some of the menu items than the waiter. I still had a lot to learn about her.

A jazz band sat in the corner, playing as the food was delivered to the table, and we ate, making small talk as if the most momentous thing that had happened to me recently wasn't sitting there, squeezing my hand.

All I wanted was to get her home and into bed.

We were eating chocolate cake for dessert when the music picked up the pace. Mum and Dad turned to watch the band. I leaned over, nuzzling Maddy's neck.

"Careful. I might think you're after something," she whispered.

"You might be right." I laughed, touching the outside of her skirt, right at the apex of her legs. If she were panty-free, this would drive her nuts.

"Stop that. You have to wait until later."

"Oh, I expect to get a lot later. Madeleine." Our faces were inches away from each other, and I grinned at that look on her face. If I were reading it correctly, she'd be hot and ready to go when we got back to my place.

"You know, it's kind of hot when you call me that," she whispered, placing her hand over mine, and pushing it between her legs.

"You look like a Madeleine tonight. And like you want to be really naughty." My fingers pressed her skirt right up and I swear her eyes rolled back in her head.

"Oh crap. You are such an arse."

"Why is that, Madeleine?"

I jumped as my mother coughed, and I looked over at her smirking at me. "I guess it's getting late," she said.

Maddy yawned, pulling her hand away from me to pat her mouth. "It is. I'm not used to being up at this time of night."

I lost it, bursting out laughing to Maddy's horror. Mum and Dad were both laughing and Maddy frowned, pinching my arm.

"Sorry." I grabbed her hand, tracing lines on the back of it with my thumb.

"Maddy, you don't need to worry about impressing us. Andrew

hasn't told us a lot, but he wouldn't be spending time with you if you weren't special. I do know that much," Mum said.

Maddy blushed, her shoulders relaxing as if the weight of the world had just been lifted from them.

"Your mum seems like a good person," Dad said, as if to back up Mum's words. "Takes someone special to run a house like she does."

"Thank you," Maddy said, "she works really hard."

"I'm sure she does. Sounds like you do too, from what Andrew has told us." He smiled at her with that warm fatherly smile of his.

She looked down at the table and shrugged. "I just work in retail, it's nothing too exciting."

"Maybe not, but it's not easy either. Andrew says you have an ear for music. I used to play in a band before we had Andrew."

The sound of my fork hitting the china plate echoed through the restaurant. "Seriously?" I stared at my father. Who was this man?

"Your father used to play guitar. When I fell pregnant with you, he decided that he needed to find a job and take life a bit more seriously. I understood, but it was such a shame. He decided it was better not to have musical instruments in the house in case they were too much of a temptation. He didn't want any distractions from our new life." My mother gazed at my father with such adoration, my stomach flipped. I'd always loved the way they looked at each other. It was the kind of look I wanted from someone I loved for the rest of my life.

"I can't imagine ever giving it up totally," Maddy said. Her eyes were full of sorrow, as if this were just something she couldn't comprehend. Neither could I; I'd never heard any of this before. "I've got a guitar at home if you want to play."

Dad grinned. "It's been years. I've probably forgotten how. Do you play too?"

Only the sun would have been brighter than Maddy's smile at that point. "I do. But I'm more violin. I always wanted to join an orchestra."

My temple pulsed, as if it were about to explode with all this new knowledge. Maddy had told me she played some instruments; I never knew she wanted a career in music. With what I'd just found out about my father, this was some crazy night.

"Come back to our place, and we'll jam." Now she'd found something in common with Dad, her confidence had grown.

Dad looked at Mum, who nodded. "Sounds great. I'll just pay the bill and we'll get out of here."

Maddy stared at him. "You're paying the bill?"

Dad looked at me, and then back at her, brow furrowed in confusion. "Yes, that was the plan."

Maddy sighed, patting my father on the hand. "I would have ordered the more expensive dishes if I'd known that." She couldn't keep the look up, and her face melted back into that beautiful smile while Dad roared with laughter.

"I like this girl, Andrew," he said, grinning at me.

I squeezed Maddy's hand. "I like her too," I said.

SEVENTEEN

I LIKED her a lot more later on, with her ankles over my shoulders. She'd played her violin while Dad played guitar for the first half hour, and then sang along with him for the rest of the time they spent. While I'd heard the beautiful music she could make with her violin, I'd never heard her sing before, each note making me want her more and more. Her voice was soft and seductive.

As much as I loved seeing my parents again, and the bond they'd created with Maddy in one evening, I couldn't wait for them to leave so I could be alone with my girl.

As soon as we waved them goodbye, I chased her up the stairs and back to my room.

No sooner had we gotten inside, I pressed her up against the door, sealing her mouth with mine, pulling her skirt up until I could slip my hand under it. A moan escaped her lips as I stroked her, pressed my fingers into her, my thumb grazing her clit. As her knees buckled, I caught her, scooping her up and into my arms, and carrying her to the bed.

She gazed up at me, her eyes full of emotion with just a touch of uncertainty. While we'd spent a lot of time in bed together, it had never been like this. We'd never had an evening like this, where she just seemed to fit into place, just like part of my family.

As it was, she'd swept me away, and I'd thrown all caution to the wind as we wrapped ourselves in each other night after night. Now, it was as if the final piece fell into place, and my heart soared as we just looked at each other, searching each other's souls for something deeper.

"Maddy," I whispered. I put my hand to her face, running my thumb across her lip. She closed her eyes, her breathing becoming ragged at a simple touch.

I had to taste her lips, and I claimed her mouth in one swift movement, feeling her kiss just as urgent as mine.

Each button on her blouse came undone in my fingers as I worked my way down, pulling it back to expose her smooth, alabaster skin. Now I had to taste that skin, and I leaned over, brushing my lips against her stomach as I reached up to stroke her breasts through the bra I'd been surprised she wore.

Never had I wanted her more, and I'd be damned if I'd ever make a mistake with her again.

The guttural sound she made as I pulled her skirt down, spreading her legs and possessing her with my tongue made me harder than I ever thought possible.

She was mine.

I CLOSED MY EYES, pulling her close. Her fingers stroked my chest with that gentle touch I'd come to adore, and I knew more than ever that this was it. In this crazy world of mine, I'd managed to find someone to care for, maybe even to love.

"Something's different," she whispered. I kissed her tenderly, sharing a smile, our eyes locking.

"You were amazing tonight. I loved listening to you, I loved how you got on so well with my father."

Maddy cocked an eyebrow. "I'm amazing every night. It's just taken you a while to notice." The grin that spread across her lips lit up her face.

"I noticed." I brushed her lips with mine, wanting the contact. "I thought I knew everything about you, but there appears to be so much more that I had no idea about."

She rolled her eyes. "Nothing that you needed to know about."

"You don't think I want to know your hopes and dreams? Maddy, listening to you tonight was indescribable. The sound you make with your violin ..."

Her nails scraped against my skin. I gasped when she planted her lips on my neck, sucking gently, and I lost myself all over again, distracting me from any thought I had as the blood rushed to other parts of my body. All for her—only for her.

IT WAS THE SAME DREAM, the one I'd dreamed a million times, or so it seemed. Over and over it played in my head, as if trying to seek some alternative ending, some different resolution.

But it was always the same.

"*She loved helping me. I'm sure she understood.*"

"*But did you explain to her?*"

Charlie shook her head, the tears rolling down her cheeks as what she had done sunk in. "*I didn't mean to hurt her. I love her.*"

"*I do too. You two are the most important people to me in the world. Do you think I wouldn't act in Rowan's best interests?*"

Out of nowhere, she pushed at me hard, and I staggered backwards.

"*I think sometimes you're selfish, and you only think of your best interests. Leave Rowan alone.*"

I rolled my eyes, exasperated at the whole conversation. I'd already warned Kyle away from Rowan, not that he would pay any attention to me.

"Screw you. You don't care what I have to say." She was out the door before I could stop her.

The bright summer light hit me as I ran out the door after her. She never ran, terrified of not being able to catch her breath, scared of the asthma attacks she'd suffered in her youth. Now, she took off and I struggled for a moment to keep up with her. Me, who went to the gym three times a week and kept fit.

"Charlie," I called. We were already a distance from the house and I was worried that she'd push herself too far. She stumbled, falling to her knees as I caught up with her, and to my horror, she wheezed as she pulled on my leg.

"You need to calm down," I whispered.

"I ... can't ... catch ..." She didn't finish her sentence, gasping for breath as I bent down to pick her up. I needed to get her back to the cabin, back to her medication.

All her things flew everywhere as she sat, watching. I emptied her suitcase on the bed, praying to find her inhaler, the phone in my hand as I called emergency services.

Trying to calm her, while screaming for an ambulance, her face reddening with the effort needed just to find that elusive breath.

No sign of the inhaler, and I threw the phone on the bed, hitting the speaker button so we still had contact with the outside world, cradling my beloved Charlie as her quest for breath failed. I wouldn't let her speak; she couldn't give up more of the precious oxygen that kept her alive.

Her big blue eyes were filled with sorrow, and we shared more love in that moment than a lifetime.

I woke to big brown eyes looking at me, Maddy's soft lips kissing away the tears on my cheeks, her soft voice telling me I'd been crying out for Charlie.

"I'm sorry, I'm so sorry," I whispered. I'd practically told her I was falling in love with her and now I was crying for my dead wife.

Good one, Andrew.

"You have nothing to be sorry for. I can be strong for you just as you are strong for me. I know when I'm with you that I'm safe, which is more than I can say about anyone else I've ever been with." She smiled just a little, enough to give me the reassurance that I hadn't upset her.

I reached up to touch her hair, like golden silk beneath my fingers. My heart beat hard, and I pulled her down roughly to kiss the lips that had given me that security.

This was me, falling apart and coming back together all in the space of a moment. It was as if I'd been frozen, numb to all that went on around me, and now I felt everything.

And it was all because of her.

EIGHTEEN

AT THE END of the month, I went to see Steve. Steve had been my counsellor right through my prison time and had heard all about Charlie and Rowan. I didn't have to keep up the sessions, but they'd helped so much, I wanted to go. Steve was a good guy who had helped me find myself again through the mess that had become my life.

This was the first time I'd been to his office; every other meeting had been in the prison, and I found myself outside an old building, reminiscent of Carly's boarding house—one of those old Victorian style houses, which was in need of a repaint, moss growing on the eaves of the house.

He grinned when he answered the door, clearly happy to see me on the other side of the fence. We'd had so many chats over the last three years—he knew my state of mind better than anyone. I considered him a friend.

We sat in the sunshine on the back deck. There was a small garden, full of fragrant flowers. Every flower reminded me of Charlie, the forbidden, as far as she was concerned.

"Tell me about Maddy," Steve said, sitting back in his chair.

"It's all been really sudden, but we're having fun together. She's so vibrant, and beautiful, and sweet. We're good for each other, I think."

He smiled. "Do you think moving so quickly is good?"

"To be honest, I have no idea, but it feels right at the moment. We're both happy with whatever it is, and my parents loved her when they came for a visit. I've told her everything—she knows what happened, what I did, and how much I regret it."

He was franticly scribbling, and I made a mental note to one day ask for all my records to see what he really thought.

"It felt more like friends with benefits than a boyfriend-girlfriend kind of thing at first, and then grew. If anything, I'm scared of breaking her heart." That was my biggest fear, having let Maddy in so quickly.

Now he looked up at me, his steely grey eyes taking in my expression. If I lay it on the line to anyone, it needed to be him. "Why do you think that?"

"She's had her problems too. Her father was an alcoholic who smacked her mother around, and hit Maddy. Sometimes I wonder if two damaged people are really going to make anything work."

He leaned forward, taking a sip out of his water glass on the table. Now I had him thinking. I'd seen a lot more of this in the early days, where as we'd been chatting more like friends.

"Do you want to make it work?"

I paused, looking at him for the moment as I pondered the question. I'd been so carried away with my developing feelings for Maddy, I hadn't thought about the long-term. My reply had been flippant, without the thought behind it that needed to be there.

"I do. We just seem to fit. She gets that I'm still struggling with Charlie's death, and she has her own nightmares. She came on strong in the beginning, but underneath all that bravado is a sensitive, sweet girl who just needs her emotional needs met. We're different, but the same."

He nodded. "I'm glad you're happy. But, as always, if there's anything you need to talk about, I'm here. Feel free to bring her along too some day. I'd love to meet the girl that's put that smile on your face."

I laughed. "That obvious, huh?"

"The second I mentioned her name, you brightened up. I think it's good for you to find someone to share your feelings with that isn't me."

That made me laugh harder. I'd been feeling the same way. Plus, the sex was amazing. Not that he needed to know that.

"SO, DID YOU TALK ABOUT ME?"

Maddy sat across the other side of the table, waving her fork in the air, her eyebrows raised in anticipation..

"We did as a matter of fact. I told Steve I'd met this crazy girl who won't leave me alone."

She grinned, poking her tongue at me.

"And I wouldn't have it any other way." I finished, lifting my foot and rubbing it against her bare leg.

She giggled, going back to her dinner. I loved the the routine we'd settled into, sharing meals and our evenings together.

It had been a long time since I'd been this happy. More than anything, I wanted it to last.

NINETEEN

I PULLED in to park just outside the house when my mobile rang. The number wasn't familiar at all, and I closed my eyes for just a second, crossing my fingers that it was about a job.

"Andrew Carmichael?" a man's voice said.

"Yes?"

"It's Damon Spears. We had an interview a couple of weeks ago?"

"Oh, yes."

Holy shit, it's Kim's boss.

"I need to talk to you about the job you interviewed for ..."

I bounced in the door, grabbing Maddy as I went past and landing on the couch with her on my lap.

"What on earth has gotten into you?" she asked, laughing.

"You," I said, raising her tank top, pulling it over her head and cupping her lace-covered breasts in my hands. She hadn't been home long enough to remove the bra she wore to work. I pulled her to me, planting kisses in the cleft of her cleavage, running my hands up her back.

She giggled, and I unclipped her bra. Her breasts spilled out, and I ran my tongue over one nipple. She shivered, her hips thrusting towards me.

"Seriously. What has gotten into you?" She pulled my head out from just under her breasts where I was nipping at her skin, revelling in the smell and taste of it.

"I got a job." I waggled my eyebrows at her, grinning at her obvious delight as she squealed.

"That's awesome. Congratulations, babe," she said, kissing me tenderly.

"Three-month trial, then a salary increase to a decent amount. I can find a nice place to live, really get on with rebuilding my life."

A shadow crossed her face as she looked away, sliding off my lap.

"What is it?" I grabbed her arm before she ran, pulling her back to me, studying her face to see what was going on.

"You're going to move out?" She could barely look at me, raising her eyes, but hiding behind her lashes.

"I didn't plan on staying here forever. It's awesome that your mother offered me this place—I appreciate it more than I can say, but I need my independence. I want more."

My grasp weakened, and she tried to pull away again. I stood, grabbing her in my arms and pulling her in tight to my chest.

"What's this about, Maddy?"

"Are you going to leave me behind?"

Her breathing was rapid, and I rubbed her back.

"Did I say that?"

She looked up at me with tear-filled eyes, shaking her head. "No."

"So why do you think I would do that? I'm happy with what we have. That doesn't have to change if I'm not in the same house as you."

I cupped her face, pulling her lips to mine. "When I said I want more, I'm talking about you and me too. Finding a job and having the money to find a place of my own is one thing. It wouldn't be complete without you. If you're up for it, I want you to come with me."

Her arms were around my neck, hugging me tight. "I'm up for it. I'm so proud of you."

I buried my face in her hair, planting little kisses under her ear. "I'm so excited, and I'm glad you're here to share this with me."

She jumped up, hooking herself around my waist and I laughed, lowering her gently onto her back on the couch. As usual, she had no underwear on beneath her skirt, and I plunged my tongue into her, teasing her while she squealed with delight.

I unbuttoned my pants, pulling them down towards my ankles, almost tripping over as I knelt back on the couch. She was so beautiful, her long, blonde hair falling everywhere and those painted nails scratching at her thighs as she played with the hem of her skirt, teasing me. But I needed no teasing.

I pulled a condom from my back pocket, rolling it on, and with one hard thrust I was inside her. She wrapped those long legs around my back, pulling me into her. Maddy's eyes twinkled with delight as we moved together.

"See this? This is what I don't want to give up," I whispered.

"Just this?"

"All of this."

I rolled off the couch and onto my back. She laughed as she straddled me, moving her hips, making me growl as I stroked her thighs.

She bent over, kissing me, and I pulled her in tight. These past few weeks had meant so much; I couldn't give her up.

Don't say it, you'll sound like a crazy person.

"I like this too," she said, thrusting one last time as I groaned my release.

She collapsed, laughing, and I rolled to my side as we both caught our breath.

"You can do that any time," I said.

"I fully intend to. If you get a new place we'll have to christen the bed and the floor and the couch, and maybe the kitchen table."

I laughed. "That's an awful lot of christening."

"Just as well you're fit. Although you are older than me. Are you sure you can keep up?"

I rolled over, stroking her arm and kissing her. "I'm sure I can try."

She grinned. "That'll do."

TWENTY

I STOOD outside the building and took a deep breath. With any luck, this was the start of a new career for me. The next step to rebuilding my life.

Opening the door, I stepped inside. Damon waited just inside and greeted me with a big smile, shaking my hand.

"Nervous?" he asked.

"More than I care to admit."

"Come on, I'll show you round."

He led me on a tour of the building, and as we passed the kitchen, I spotted Kim. I hadn't thought about how awkward things might be between us, and my heart pounded as we approached.

"And of course, you know Kim," Damon said.

I attempted a smile, and Kim turned, smiling sweetly at us.

"Hey, Andrew," she said, as if our night out had never happened.

"Hi," I said.

"Glad to see you got the job. I sung your praises."

The unease I'd felt began to disappear, grinned. "Thanks."

Damon took me to my new desk, and I spent the morning acquainting myself with my computer, getting things set up the way I wanted. He was easing me into the job, and I had a thick wad of paperwork to take a look through, see how things were done.

At lunchtime, I opened my lunchbox and burst out laughing. Maddy had packed it when she'd made her lunch in the morning, and she'd cut my sandwiches into quarters and included some kids fruit jellies. "The cheek," I muttered under my breath.

"Looks like you've got your school lunch there." Kim's voice came from behind and I laughed again, nodding.

"My girlfriend has a real sense of humour."

Kim perched herself on the corner of the desk, sandwich in hand, looking over my food.

"Girlfriend, huh? You sorted things out, or is this a new one?"

I shook my head. "Same one. We managed to get our shit together."

She looked pensive. "I'm happy for you. I mean it. After everything, it's good that you're happy."

"I was worried things might be uncomfortable between us."

Kim shrugged. "You were still a great candidate for the job. Life's too short for holding grudges. Besides, with you being here, I can keep an eye on you in case things don't work out with you and your girlfriend."

I laughed. At least things were okay between us.

What made me happier than anything these days was the thought of Maddy waiting for me to get home. She was well under my skin now, and things were serious.

Maddy was so refreshing, never holding anything back. She spoke her mind, and what an amazing mind that was. So down to earth, and smart, hellishly smart, and she had no real idea just how phenomenal she was.

All the family drama she'd had to deal with had really screwed her up. This was a young woman who could really go places, but had no one to tell her that, no one to give her that push to succeed. Her mother had done her best, but battling family issues had taken its toll on both Carly and Maddy. Maybe I could help Maddy find her way.

I got to the foot of the stairs; still no sign of Maddy. I could only assume she'd be skulking around upstairs, waiting for me to come home. I had to admit, I kinda liked that. It was like domestic bliss, but without the final commitment of living together.

A woman's scream pierced the air, and I turned in the direction of the sound. Bob stumbled past, looking towards the noise too. He grabbed my arm as I began to move.

"Old man Jones is back; he's taking care of some business. I'd steer clear if I were you."

"What the hell does that mean, *taking care of some business?*"

He sighed. "He's come back looking for money, from what I understand. That's what he was yelling about earlier. I've called the police."

I yanked my arm away. "Has there been more screaming?"

He nodded. "I think they're all arguing. I'm not getting into it; I won't go back inside for anything. You'd be best to get up to your room. Last thing you want is the cops sniffing around."

Another scream shattered the otherwise quiet house, and I dropped the grocery bags where I stood, running towards Maddy and her mother's rooms.

The door was locked, and I rattled the handle franticly, trying to get in. Whatever happened to me didn't matter. Only Maddy mattered.

Raised voices were muffled by the door, both a male voice and Maddy's, increasing in volume. Backing up, I shoulder-charged the door. In the state of disrepair the building was in, the door gave way to me, the frame cracking loudly as I broke the lock.

Carly cowered in the corner as the man I assumed was her husband stood in the centre of the room. He didn't even look up at me as he stood over Maddy, screaming at her to give him whatever money she had.

"You stupid slut. There must be something."

"There's nothing." She gasped through her tears and all I saw was

Charlie, taking her last breath in my arms, struggling to breathe through her sadness, then the fear of dying.

Before I could get to him, he raised his arm, backhanding her across the face and sending her backwards into the kitchen counter. She hit it with a thud, falling to the floor.

"Maddy," I yelled.

He turned, and I greeted him with a fist to the jaw. It hit with a resounding crack as he went down. I didn't know if it was teeth or jaw I had broken, and I didn't care. They could send me back to jail for the rest of my life—saving Maddy would be worth it.

I ran to Maddy. She lay still, lifeless, and my heart leapt to my throat as I felt for a pulse.

"She's not breathing," I said.

"What do I do?" Carly shrieked. She stood behind me now, her hands fisted.

"Call an ambulance. Get them here as fast as you can."

"Please help her." She was crying now, but my focus had to be on Maddy. I couldn't lose her too.

I tilted her head back, looking for any sign of breathing.

"Maddy, don't you dare do this to me," I whispered.

With no signs of life, I started chest compressions, closing my eyes and praying for the first time in longer than I could remember. She had to be okay. She just had to.

One—two—three.

Carly made the call. She'd sorted herself out enough to get through it, and I just hoped they could get here fast.

One—two—three.

Don't you dare.

I was running on adrenalin, conjuring up some deeply hidden memory from high school. We'd spent a day doing CPR training, and I hoped more than anything I was getting it right.

One—two—three.

Maddy.

Finishing compressions, I went back to check for breathing,

acting quickly to tilt her head and pinch her nose, just the way I'd learned. Each breath I hoped would be the one to bring her back to me, that she would open her eyes and I'd be able to hold her, love her the way she needed to be loved.

An eternity passed until she finally took that breath by herself and I let go, listening to her inhale and exhale, watching her chest rise and fall. Her eyes flickered open, and I was overjoyed to see her awake, even if she did look confused.

"Maddy," I whispered. She pushed herself up to sit, and just stared at me.

"What happened?"

"You got hit and smacked into the bench. You weren't breathing, baby. I was so scared."

She looked over at the man on the floor, and a look crossed her face that told me she remembered. "Dad came back looking for money. We told him we didn't have any, but he kept yelling, and yelling." Her breathing accelerated now, the upset evident on her face.

"Maddy," I said again.

Maddy looked back at me, meeting my gaze and let out a big sob. She flung her arms around my neck and I just held her, breathing into her hair as she cried.

"Ambulance and police are on the way." Carly's voice was faint behind us.

I pried Maddy's arms off my neck, holding her at a close distance. Tears ran down her face as she took in my every feature, my eyes focused on the spot her father had hit. Her skin was red and blotchy, she'd have a big bruise.

Her lips crashed onto mine as I held her tight, and she kissed me as if it were our last time. I ran my fingers through her hair, feeling its softness, stroking her face as she kept kissing me, not wanting to let go.

My chest tightened as I thought about losing her. She was safe, but now we'd come this far, how cruel it would be to be torn apart.

"I'll just go outside," Carly said.

Maddy's tongue pushed into my mouth and I pushed back; clearly she didn't want to waste any more time, and if it weren't for the fact that I was vaguely aware of the police being on their way, I would have stripped her and taken her there and then.

I pulled away gently, Maddy's eyes following me intently as I released my grip on her.

"Maddy, if I end up back inside ..."

"You won't. They'll understand. They have to."

I sighed. "If I do, I want you to know how much you mean to me. When I got out, I wanted a new start, and I wasn't looking for anything, but what we have? I wouldn't trade it for anything."

"I want more. I always wanted more."

I shook my head, laughing. "I know, and I want to say I am so glad I met you. You've been so good for me, and I adore you. I hope you know that."

She lifted her hand to her face, wincing as she tentatively touched the reddened skin. "Ugh, this bruise is going to make me so ugly. Will you still like me then?"

I laughed, stroking the other side of her face. "Only you could come up with something like that. I'm crazy about you. There you go, happy now?"

"I think you're pretty nice too." She leaned over, brushing her lips against mine. "Actually, really nice."

"It's kind of you to say that."

"I'm a kind girl."

I grinned. She really was. And if this was to be our last moment for a while, at least I knew she felt the same way.

Footsteps behind me didn't register until I was pulled to my feet. Moment of truth. It was time to face the police.

AFTER WHAT FELT LIKE HOURS, I made it back to the boarding house. Carly stood with a handyman, who was fixing the damage I'd done when I'd pushed through the door.

"I'll pay for whatever you need doing," I said to her.

She jumped, not having heard me come in, and turned, flinging her arms around my neck. I laughed. "What's all this for?"

"You saved us. Maddy could have been killed if you weren't there."

"You're okay now. I just really want to get some sleep."

She let go of me, cocking her head as she took me in. "Are you in trouble? I told them everything I could, told them you were defending us."

I shook my head. "They had to get to the bottom of it. When they heard the whole story, it was clear I was looking after you two and stopped him from hurting you more. The police said there were also several arrest warrants out for your ex, more than enough to keep him busy."

"Good. It'll keep him away from here. At least, for a while."

"I'm just glad Maddy is safe. I couldn't lose her."

"She loves you; I hope you know that. She's good at hiding her feelings, that one, but I can see it clear as day."

"I love her too. Where is she?"

She sighed. "The paramedic wanted her to go to hospital for observation, but she insisted on staying and waiting for you. She didn't want to be down here, not with everything that's happened. She's up in your room."

"Thanks, Carly."

Carly nodded, smiling.

I turned towards the stairs, climbing them two at a time. My future was at the top—at least, I hoped that was the way Maddy saw things too. I hadn't planned on falling in love and settling down so soon, but if she would have me, I'd be hers. No looking back.

She was lying in bed, her eyes closed, and her breathing steady.

I'd never heard anything so beautiful in all my life after seeing her so still, lifeless.

I stripped, sliding in to bed beside her, and pulling her into my arms. It didn't matter whether we made love or not: she was with me, and safe.

Maddy stirred, pressing her body against mine "I thought you were never coming home," she mumbled.

"It's not that late. I hear you were told to go to the hospital," I said sternly.

She looked up at me with sleepy eyes, and pouty lips.

"I was more worried about you. I didn't want them to take you away from me."

I sighed. "Maddy, I wouldn't have had any control over that. Can you imagine what it would have been like for me to end up back in there and find you'd died in your sleep because your injuries needed attention?"

She buried her nose in my shoulder, as if trying to burrow into the bed. "I wanted to be here when you came home."

"What if I hadn't come home?"

Maddy pushed herself up. Her brow furrowed, and she frowned as she looked at me. "I don't know what I'd do."

"I don't know what I'd do either. You're what keeps me going right now, Maddy Jones. If I lost you, there would be no point to me."

"Do you want me to go to the hospital, then?" She pouted.

"Just cuddle up with me and get some sleep. We'll go and get you looked at again in the morning. If I have to, I'll watch you like a damn hawk."

She snuggled down beside me again, smiling before a yawn took her over. "I like the idea of you watching me."

"I love you, Maddy."

At that she sat back up again, licking her lips, the smile turning into a grin. "Say again?"

"I love you, Maddy."

"I must be dreaming. I thought you said you loved me." She

flopped back down again. Half asleep, she still had far more energy than I did.

"I do. Very much. Now, come here and let's get some sleep. I think we both need it."

She sighed contentedly, tangling herself up in me. I stroked her hair as I closed my eyes.

"I love you too," she whispered.

I could stay up all night listening to her breathe, it sounded so good.

TWENTY-ONE

THREE MONTHS.

The moment had arrived, and my nervousness over this job progressing past the trial had grown and grown. Maddy kept reassuring me that everything would be fine, that I was doing a great job. She'd seen just how much I'd buried myself in my work, determined to make a good impression. I always made time for her.

I'd been distracted by the work, and while she had practically moved in with me, Maddy still kept her room downstairs so she could let me concentrate. She'd seemed distracted herself at times, but had insisted nothing was wrong. I just thought she was trying to let me get on with it.

Damon called me into his office. Butterflies tormented my stomach, my head aching from the stress. I didn't think I had anything to fear, but mine was a kind of unique situation. I doubted anyone else I worked with had ever been convicted for kidnapping.

"Andrew, I wanted to talk to you about your work," he said, not giving away a thing.

"Sure. I'm really enjoying it. It's been good to get back into the swing of things."

He smiled. "It shows; you've done a great job. So ..."

Reaching across the desk, he placed a small pile of papers in front of me.

"Your new contract. Permanent and the salary slightly more than discussed. Take it and read it over before you sign it, and I hope you do sign it."

"Thank you so much. I don't know what to say."

He grinned. "You deserve it. Go out and celebrate tonight, and no taking any work home."

I picked up the papers, hardly believing what I held in my hand. This was it, my ticket to the next step of my life. I couldn't wait to get home and share my good news with Maddy.

ALL I COULD SEE when I walked in the door was her bent over the oven door. If it hadn't been dangerous, I would have gone up and groped her, but the oven was on and the room was warm from whatever was cooking.

"Hey," I said.

She closed the oven door, turning towards me, a huge grin on her face.

"How was your day?" Maddy asked.

"You cooked dinner; that makes today pretty eventful. Oh, and my job was made permanent."

She squealed, leaping at me, hooking her legs around my hips. I squeezed her thighs as she kissed me, and she growled before letting go.

"That's awesome. I'm so proud of you."

"More money than I thought, too. This is it, Maddy." I wandered past her, moving towards the oven. "What's for dinner?"

"I couldn't wait for you to get home. I was starving and I really felt like mac and cheese."

In the oven was the biggest casserole dish I had ever seen, full of pasta.

"How hungry were you?" I asked.

Her eyes darted as if she were thinking of what she could say. "I thought it would make good leftovers for lunch."

"Gonna be a lot of lunches out of this lot," I muttered, closing the oven door.

She grabbed my hands, pulling me to the couch. "It'll be ready in a minute. Sit down, and put your feet up."

"I could get used to this," I said. I put my feet up on the coffee table.

"Get your feet off there," Maddy said, as if channelling Mum.

I laughed, beckoning her to join me. She sat beside me, wagging her index finger.

"You have no idea what a turn-off it is when you act like my mother," I said.

Maddy's eyes grew wide, and she exploded with laughter, grabbing my arm. "Sorry."

"I'll take my feet off the table, anything you want." I pulled her roughly onto my lap, pressing my lips to hers.

"I have to get up before dinner burns," she said.

"But *I'm* burning," I said, blanking my face to look serious.

She rolled her eyes, laughing, and shook her head. Pushing herself off my lap she got up and I watched as she walked back to the oven, wolf whistling as she bent over.

SHE ATE with the greatest gusto I'd ever seen, inhaling three helpings before admitting defeat.

"So ... not so much for lunches, then?" I teased.

Maddy rolled her eyes as she threw a dishcloth at me from the counter.

"Sorry. I've just never known you to eat so much. Must be all the working out you've done lately." I grinned. While I went to the gym most days, she hated exercise. Unless it was of the horizontal kind, and occasionally vertical. We'd been doing a lot of both.

"I dreamed about that all day. All I wanted was pasta and cheese."

She turned on the tap, running the water for the dishes. I stood, moving behind her and reaching over to turn it off.

"What are you doing?" she asked.

"Fulfilling the craving I've had all day."

I placed my hands on her hips, turning her toward me. She smiled that warm smile at me, the one that started at her lips and travelled up to her eyes—the one that told me she was truly happy.

In one swift move, I lifted her off the floor and threw her over my shoulder. She squealed as I carried her to the bed, tipping her back and lowering her until she lay in the middle, laughing, so full of joy.

"Now, we have dessert," I said.

IT WAS LATE. Once we started, we didn't want to stop, but the practical reality of working the next day brought us to a halt.

We snuggled up to sleep when Maddy became emotional.

She buried her face in my chest, her shoulders shaking as she cried.

"What's going on? What's wrong?" I whispered, stroking her shoulders.

"Do you really love me?" She sobbed, raising her tear-stained face to me.

"You know I do. Maddy, I'm crazy about you."

"I'm not ... I'm not just a stand in for Charlie?"

I frowned, running my fingers through her hair and pulling her head back towards me. "No. There's only one Maddy. I loved Charlie, but she's gone. You're whom I love now. What's causing all this?"

She sobbed on my shoulder, burying her nose into my skin. I stroked her shoulder.

What's brought this on?

"Nothing." She said it in the same tone she usually said "fine" in, which meant something was bugging her.

"Seriously, baby. As much as I loved Charlie, that part of my life died when she did. I might not have realised it at the time, but it did. Now, I am head over heels for this gorgeous woman who drives me crazy, but in a good way. I wouldn't change anything for the world."

I held her until she fell asleep, and I stroked her back, wondering where her outburst had come from. Things had been great between us, and I hoped they kept going the way they had been. Maddy put up such a front in the face of dealing with so many hard things from her past, but I saw through that, through to the gentle, sensitive young woman who lurked below the surface. She couldn't be more different to Charlie if she tried.

Charlie had worn her heart on her sleeve—you always knew where you stood with her. Her biggest struggle had been keeping our love from Rowan—she'd fought that every day. Maddy buried everything until it built to the point of explosion. Oh, she'd put on a face and pretend things didn't bother her, but deep down, she felt it all.

TWENTY-TWO

SHE WAS off-colour in the morning, complaining of a headache and feeling tired.

"Call in sick. It's probably why you were so miserable last night," I said. "Sounds like you're coming down with something."

Maddy shrugged, pulling the pillow over her head. "Good idea." Her muffled voice was weary, and I patted her on the arm.

"Sleep it off. I'll bring home dinner tonight. Screw cooking."

She mumbled her agreement, and I showered and dressed for work before leaving, floating on air because my girl loved me and I loved her and everything was right with the world despite her illness.

By the time I got home, she'd moved as far as the couch, and I bent to kiss her, waving a pizza box under her nose.

"That smells gross."

"I love you too," I said, sitting beside her, and opening the box on the coffee table. I breathed in the smell of pepperoni and oregano.

She picked up the remote, changing channels to the news and we sat in silence watching the world's events while I ate.

"Sure you don't want some?" I asked.

She shook her head, her lips downturned. It had been a long time since I'd seen her looking so glum.

"Why don't you have a shower and go to bed? I'll change the sheets while you're washing so it's nice and fresh if you've slept all day."

Maddy leaned on my arm, resting her head on my shoulder. "You're so good to me."

"You're pretty good to me, too."

"I think I'll have a shower and get changed. Maybe we can find something to watch on TV."

I licked my fingers, removing the grease from the pizza and reached up to touch her face. "That sounds good. Let me know if you need anything."

"Getting rid of that would be a good start. It's still gross." She pointed at the pizza and I nodded.

"Anything you want."

She stood, slouching as she walked to the bathroom.

I finished what I was eating and went to the fridge, placing the pizza on the top shelf. No point wasting it. Once she felt better she'd probably want some.

After changing the sheets, I cracked open a beer, returning to the couch to watch the sports news. Some day, and not too far away, we'd have a proper house of our own, with a bigger television than the twenty-three-inch screen I currently had.

It couldn't come soon enough.

I put the beer on the coffee table, and lay down on the couch, closing my eyes for just a moment. I jumped, waking when my feet were lifted from the couch as Maddy returned, and I opened my eyes to see her standing over me, that glum expression still on her face.

"Feel better?" I said.

She nodded, but I didn't believe her. The light that usually radiated from her was dull, lifeless, and I just wanted to hold her and fix whatever was going on.

I patted the couch beside me and she sat down. "Want a beer?" I asked.

Maddy shook her head. "I just want to watch whatever mindless programme is on and then go to bed."

"Whatever you want, babe."

We sat in silence, even while *Grey's Anatomy* was on. It was her favourite show, and she was usually full of commentary about who was supposed to be together, who shouldn't be together, who was screwing who. But tonight, nothing—just the silence.

"You're quiet," I said, leaning my head on Maddy's shoulder.

She sniffed, and I raised my head to look at her. Tears rolled down her face, and I reached up to wipe them with my fingers.

"Maddy? What's wrong?"

She shook her head, taking a deep breath with a sob in the middle.

"Maddy?"

She swallowed hard as she looked up at me, new tears welling to replace the ones I'd removed.

"Holy crap, Maddy. I need to know what is wrong. You are scaring the shit out of me right now."

She twisted her mouth, obviously trying to find a way to tell me what she was so clearly struggling with. She looked at the floor, and my stomach flipped in concern.

"I'm pregnant," she whispered.

"Oh."

That was it; that was all I could manage. I hadn't expected her to come out with that, and I didn't know how she expected me to react, but in an instant she was on her feet, fleeing towards the door.

"Maddy," I called, pushing myself up to run after her.

She flew down the stairs, into her mother's rooms and shut the door behind her. I sighed, walking down and knocking on the door.

Carly opened, looking puzzled. "She just came straight through here and into her room. What's wrong? Are you two fighting? Please tell me you're not, because she hasn't been as big a pain in the butt with you around."

I shook my head. "I need to talk to her."

"Come in and sort it out. No yelling at each other though."

"Yes, Ma'am," I said. She shook her head, rolling her eyes as she walked away.

I pushed through the door to Maddy's bedroom. Maddy sat on her bed, arms folded and pulling a sour face.

"You have to let the news sink in before you decide to run away," I said, sitting on the bed beside her. "Give me more than five seconds to process it."

She stuck her bottom lip out, clearly fighting the urge to cry some more.

"I can get rid of it." She barely got the words out, loud gasps between each one.

"Maddy, I love your spirit, your independence—as if I could ever make you do anything you didn't want. Whatever you decide, I'll be there with you. You and I are practically living together as it is. Having a baby isn't going to be easy, but we'll manage either way."

Slowly, she raised her eyes until she met mine, and there was a faint smile in them. "Really?" she croaked.

"Really. If we are doing this, we need to find somewhere else to live, though. This place is no good for a baby."

I laughed as she launched herself at me, wrapping her arms around my neck. Falling backwards on the bed, I stroked her hair as she straddled me, leaning over for a kiss.

"We'll manage," I said when she let me go. "We'll find a way."

She grinned through the tears, kissing me again. "I love you, Andrew."

"Love you too. Now, we can go and finish watching your show, or we can go and tell your mother the news. Unless she's heard already."

Maddy laughed. The walls weren't exactly soundproof. There was a good chance Carly already knew she was going to be a grandmother.

Sure enough, Carly was waiting outside when we emerged, clapping her hands together.

"I guess you heard," Maddy grumbled. Carly threw her arms around Maddy, and I grinned at her excitement.

"I thought you'd be a bit crazy with me," Maddy said into her mother's neck. "We haven't been together *that* long."

Carly released Maddy, cupping her face in her hands. "Andrew's a good man, probably the best you've been involved with. He'll take care of you, sweetheart. If he didn't care, he wouldn't be down here trying to make things right."

Maddy nodded, turning towards me. "He is a good man, Mum."

WE LAY IN BED, limbs tangled together, basking in the glow of our lovemaking.

Maddy rubbed her cheek against mine, making a purring noise as I laughed. "You're happy, then?"

"You could say that," she whispered. "I felt so awful today—first morning sickness, and then not knowing how to tell you."

She was snuggled in my arms, and I kissed her softly. "You make me laugh. And you make me cry. I felt so empty, but you brought me back to life."

Maddy raised an eyebrow. "Is that from a song or something?"

"No." I laughed. "Being with you made me human again. After everything, I felt like I'd lost so much of myself, but you found me, and you loved me. Turned out to be just what I needed."

I slid my hand down to her stomach, stroking her warm skin. "You and this little one will get everything from me. You've given me so many reasons to be better. I want a future now, and I'm not dwelling in the past."

She closed her eyes, tucking her head under my chin. "I should have known you wouldn't be angry," she whispered.

Bringing my hand back up, I ran my fingers up her arm. "I could never be angry with you. Everything happens for a reason."

"I was scared you would think I did it on purpose."

"Maddy, even if you did do it on purpose, it's too late to worry about it now. Besides, this just means you're stuck with me."

She giggled, slipping her arm over me and softly pinching my back. "I think I can live with that."

As she rolled over, she took my hand, guiding it to her breast.

"Miss Jones, are you trying to tell me something?"

"No. Just keeping you close. I think I need some sleep. This whole thing has worn me out."

I snuggled in tight, spooning with Maddy as we settled in to sleep.

"Grow old with me," I whispered into her hair, not even sure she'd hear.

Of course she did; she never missed a thing. Maddy rolled onto her back, cocking an eyebrow at me.

"Did you say what I think you said?" she asked.

"I don't have a ring, but we can go shopping tomorrow. It won't be much, but I want to be with you, Maddy. For always."

"I want to be with you too," she whispered, her eyes filled with longing. I brushed my lips against hers, and she laughed against my kiss, rolling on top of me.

"But I thought you were worn out?"

Maddy laughed. Moonlight flooded in the window, and she glowed with happiness. She was just so freaking beautiful. "I think I might just need a night cap."

TWENTY-THREE

I PORED over the real estate section of the paper, looking for houses to rent. We'd definitely need a house now rather than a small place, and I wanted to find the right one. One Maddy would love.

"I don't know if I want to move." Maddy sat with her arms folded defensively, a frown etched on her face.

"I want you to," said Carly. "Not because I don't love you, but because I do. You had to live here in this run-down place because of the choices I made for you. Now you have the opportunity to do good for your child, give him or her what I couldn't."

Maddy's lower lip wobbled, and she let out a loud sob, throwing her arms around her mother's neck. "I had a great childhood."

Carly raised an eyebrow, clearly thinking of her husband and what they'd been through with him.

"In a big old house that was always threatening to fall down around our ears, surrounded by ex-prison inmates. I could have done better for you, Maddy."

She looked across at me, smiling while Maddy clung to her. "I know you'll take good care of my girl, and my grandbaby. You're a good man, Andrew."

"I hope I'm good enough," I said.

"You've done more for Maddy in a short time than anyone else has. You'll never know just how much I appreciate you."

There were tears in her eyes, and I know she meant what she said. I'd never let anything hurt Maddy, not me, not anyone else.

"I'll love and protect her forever," I said.

Carly nodded, her smile saying she knew I meant it. And I did.

"WHAT ARE we going to do after the baby comes?" Maddy asked, cuddled up with me at night.

"What do you mean?"

"How are we going to manage? All this talking about moving in to a place of our own, and I'll be off work for a while after the baby is born, but what then?"

I kissed her forehead, nuzzling her hair. "Depends on how expensive a place we get. I'm trying to find somewhere affordable, so if you decide not to go back to work you don't have to. I don't mind either way, Maddy, but I want you to have the choice."

"Mum stayed home with me. I mean, she was running this place, but she was always at home." She pulled away, looking up at me.

"If you want to do that, it's fine. I want to look after you for a while. But, we'll have to see what kind of place we can find first."

She nodded, chewing on her lower lip. "We could just stay here."

"I think your mother is going to kick us out if we don't leave. She knows you have to do something for yourself. Let's wait until after the wedding. At least there's no rush."

Satisfied, she nestled in close and I closed my eyes, ready for sleep. There was nothing but good dreams now. Maddy and the baby took care of that.

Sometime in the night, I heard the violin and smiled, even though the bed was cold. Maddy played a lullaby for our unborn child.

I sighed, drawing the blanket closer and drifted back to sleep.

"What are we going to do for the wedding?" she asked the next day.

I shrugged. I'd already been through one big dressy wedding, and had no interest in another one. But, if it was what Maddy wanted ...

"I thought we could just do the registry office. I mean, it's not like there will be heaps of people coming, and we can just have a small ceremony even with just our parents," she said.

She jumped as I laughed loudly. "I hadn't given it that much thought, Maddy, but I'm happy with whatever you want to do. Sounds perfect."

"What's so funny?" Maddy moved closer, and I pulled her onto my lap.

"What you want sounds great. Nice and quiet, and then I'll drag you off to some motel to have my wicked way with you." I stroked her thigh as I spoke, happy she'd decided that by herself.

She grinned, leaning over for a kiss. "Love it. Let's do it."

"Here, or near Mum and Dad?"

Maddy's eyes widened. Clearly the choice of venues hadn't even crossed her mind.

"What do you want?" she asked.

"Baby, I don't care. It's your special day, Maddy. I'll go wherever you want me to, do whatever you want me to. I'm happy if you're happy."

"If we get married near your parents, we can go and visit Charlie, run the whole thing past her," she said. She stood, moving to the couch, her feet on the coffee table. I would have been told off for that, but apparently it was okay if Maddy did it.

I gulped. The thought of that scared the crap out of me. Maddy was only thinking of me, but my heart beat faster thinking of Charlie's grave.

"Andrew?" She looked up from her magazine, her eyes full of worry.

I licked my lips, trying to find moisture to speak. "I love it. That's such a sweet idea."

"If we want to say goodbye to the past, we have to do it properly," she said. "Besides, I like the idea of making sure she knows you're okay."

I couldn't say anything, and moved to the couch, pulling her into my arms to thank her for being so sweet.

She really loved me.

TWENTY-FOUR

I'D VOWED to visit Charlie's grave as often as I could, but had been too scared to do so until now. Despite my life taking a new direction, I still missed her so much. I missed the way she smelled, that clean soapy scent because she couldn't wear perfume with her allergies. That deep, throaty laugh of hers. I'd muffle it with a kiss, and it would seem to hang in her chest, reverberating and making it even sexier.

And those big blue eyes of hers, the ones that would be so full of love and adoration. For so long after her death, I would have given anything to see those eyes again.

I crouched in front of the gravestone with the biggest bouquet of red roses I could afford. We'd never had flowers around the house 'just in case' but now, I gave Charlie as many as I could. It was the least I could do.

Running my fingers over her name, my chest tightened as the tears began to roll. She was buried as I wanted her to be, with my surname, Charlotte 'Charlie' Carmichael.

"God, I love you so much, Charlie. Miss you every day, babe," I whispered.

A hand rested on my shoulder, and I looked up to see Maddy.

"I know you told me I should stay in the car, but I had to be here. I have to tell her that I'm taking care of you now," she said, tears forming in her eyes.

"Thanks," I whispered, turning my head to kiss her hand.

"Charlie, this is Maddy. We're getting married, and having a baby. I wanted to tell you for myself," I said.

Maddy squeezed my shoulder. "I promise I'll take good care of him for you," she said. "I'll make sure he gets popcorn when he watches movies, and that he always wears clean socks, because you know he's terrible at changing them. I'll love him forever, Charlie. I'll make sure he's never without love again."

I couldn't say anything else, so overwhelmed with love for Maddy and Charlie in that moment. Standing, I took Maddy in my arms, hugging her tightly, and burying my nose in her neck.

"We'll come here and visit," Maddy said. "Either both of us, or you, or even just me. We'll make sure she has flowers, and I'll tell her everything you've been doing, even when I'm grumpy with you."

"You don't have to do that," I whispered.

"I know I don't. But, you loved her, and no one can replace her. Not even me. I'm just slotting in beside her, and I'm okay with that. I'm pretty sure we can share."

I grinned, lifting my head, and kissing her tenderly on the lips. "I love you so much, Maddy."

"Love you too. Can we go and get married now?" She looked down at the gravestone. "No offence, Charlie."

My heart soared as we walked back to the car. The dark clouds that had descended on Charlie's death gave way to a clear sky, and the light that came from Maddy produced the smallest of rainbows. That described Maddy to a tee. She was my rainbow.

WE DROVE past the church where Charlie and I were married, and I blew a kiss to the old place. Charlie had been so happy that day, and I had loved her, yet found so much distraction in Rowan's life.

Now, I was completely focused on my new life with Maddy—nothing from either of our pasts was going to hold us back.

We arrived at the entrance to the registrar's office, and I paused to look at Maddy.

"We're here." I said, adjusting my tie. "You look gorgeous, by the way."

Maddy pulled me over to kiss me, and I laughed against her lips. "That happens later, beautiful," I mumbled.

Hand in hand, we went into the offices, my parents and her mother right behind us. And as they watched, we swore our vows to always love one another and be together forever.

I meant every word.

Afterwards, we sat in my parents' living room where we snuggled together and I rubbed her growing belly. This was all crazy stuff, and happening so fast, but I wouldn't have changed a thing, in all the world. It had been so long since I'd felt this happy, and I revelled in the excitement.

Maddy glowed, radiating her exuberance, and I knew she'd be a little devil in bed tonight. She was in just that mood, and I couldn't wait to get my wife alone. Once we'd had dinner with our parents, we'd be off to the little motel down the road, to the room we'd booked to spend our wedding night in.

It wasn't anything flashy, but it was ours.

AND THEN WE got the most amazing wedding present we could have ever asked for, but it hurt more than I could ever tell Maddy to receive it.

Charlie's parents were unexpected visitors on our last day with Mum and Dad. They had kept in touch with me, but we hadn't seen each other since I got out. Our relationship was understandably strained—they loved Rowan as much as anyone, but they loved me too, and had supported me through the devastation of Charlie's death.

This day, though, something was different; that much was obvious from their warm reception of Maddy.

"Maddy, this is Mr and Mrs Miller, Charlie's mum and dad."

Maddy smiled. She squeezed my hand, her chest rising and falling faster than it usually did.

I squeezed back to reassure her.

Charlie's mother hugged Maddy, while Charlie's father shook my hand, and wished me all the best for our marriage.

We sat in the lounge, Mum and Dad making themselves scarce to give us some time together. These people were my family too.

"I'm sorry we didn't invite you to the ceremony," I said. "We just kept it to Mum, Dad, and Maddy's mother. We wanted to keep it low key. Especially after …"

Tears welled up in Charlie's mother's eyes, and I reached for her hand, squeezing it. "I still miss her every day. Maddy knows that, and she loves me anyway."

Charlie's mother nodded, a small smile appearing on her lips, reassured by my words. Despite my new marriage, I hadn't forgotten her daughter.

"To cut to the chase, Andrew, we have something for you." Charlie's father smiled at Maddy and I, and she touched my arm, leaning close.

"When Charlie died, we received a pay-out from the endowment policy we bought for her when she was younger. We did it for all the girls, so that they would have a retirement fund. It doubled as a life insurance policy, so on her death they paid us the sum insured."

I nodded. No money would ever be enough to replace Charlie, but I was glad for them; it would help them in their retirement.

A glance between them told me something more was in the wind. Maddy's grip tightened on my arm, and I knew she was just as curious.

"I don't really know how to say this, Andrew, but you know we consider you a son. Things went horribly wrong, but we all know Charlie was prone to asthma, and you did your best to save her and get her to the hospital in time. We can't fault you for that. I know what her death did to you."

"Thank you. I can't tell you how sorry I am to have let you down," I said. I'd said it a million times before, and every time I meant it. To my parents, and to Charlie's.

"Truth is, she was with the man she loved when she died. I couldn't ask for more than that. She was loved, and now you're out of that crazy hell you went through and have found some happiness, so we'd like to help you move forward."

I fought back the tears that were threatening, Maddy rested her head on my shoulder.

"We want to give you the insurance money. You were legally Charlie's next of kin, and if we'd transferred the policy when she turned twenty-one as we originally planned, it would have gone to you. Charlie was never very good with paperwork."

I laughed. That much was true. She was smart, and would guide me and tell me what I should do, but it was always me who ended up dealing with everything once we got together. I applied for our marriage licence, I signed our apartment lease, and I handled our finances when we merged them.

Mr Miller handed me an envelope. "It's enough to help you with a deposit on a house maybe, or a really good car. You'll need one of those, with the baby on the way."

I tucked it in my pocket, taking his hand to shake. "I don't know how to thank you."

"Don't you want to know how much it is?"

"That's not important. It just means so much that you still think of me in this way after everything that happened."

He had more compassion in his eyes than I had ever seen. "I lost my baby girl that day. I understand you more than you would know. I'm not surprised it made you crazy. Now you have Maddy and the baby to ground you. You're a good man, Andrew. From what I've seen, all of this has knocked that arrogance out of you. You always did have a chip on your shoulder."

"He still does," Maddy said, looking up and poking her tongue out at me before resting her head on my shoulder again.

Mr Miller laughed. "Well, he's your problem now. But, please keep in touch, let us know how you're getting on and if there's anything we can ever do."

"You've already done so much," she said. I turned my head, kissing the top of hers. Whatever the amount of money, it would help us without a doubt.

Her eyes widened as she opened the envelope. She'd torn it from my pocket the second they were gone, then pulled out the cheque before bursting into tears.

"Maddy?"

"It's fifty thousand dollars. Andrew. This is amazing."

I buried my face in her hair as she sobbed. "I'm sorry," she said.

"What for? You're excited. This gets us off to a good start."

She looked up at me, frowning. "It's where it came from."

"Now you know why I didn't want to open it in front of them. As much as I love having their support, I don't know if I can take it."

Maddy hugged me until I could no longer breathe. "What are you doing?" I asked

"If you want to give it back, or give it away, I won't be upset. You have to do what feels right."

I pulled at her hands until she released me. "They gave it to us because of the baby. Let's just make sure that we give our baby the best start that we can. With the money Mum and Dad are giving us, we can look at a bigger place."

"For the baby," she whispered.

"And for my wife." I pushed a stray lock back from her face, smiling at her.

She took my hand, moving it down to her stomach, the small bump that was our child warming my heart.

TWENTY-FIVE

ALMOST AS SOON AS we were back, Carly pressed us to set a date for moving out. It was time for Maddy and I to find a place of our own.

"But this is home," Maddy said, pouting.

"And it's time to start your new life with your husband," Carly said.

With the money Charlie's parents had given us, and more from Mum and Dad, we had enough to buy a small house. At least we could still stay where we were until we found a place. Carly wasn't quite kicking us out.

I was at work when Maddy called me. At first I couldn't understand what she was saying, she was sobbing so hard, and my first thought was the baby.

"Maddy? Calm down. Tell me what's going on. Are you okay?"

A mess of words came down the line, and I knew I had to be with her.

"Maddy. Are you at work?"

I heard a yes come through the sobbing, and I ran down the

corridor to Damon's office. "I need to go and get Maddy, something's happened."

He looked up. "I hope everything's okay."

"I don't know. Whatever has happened, Maddy's inconsolable. All I could get out of her was that she was at work."

He grimaced. "That doesn't sound good. Get going."

I nodded, turning towards the door and sprinting out to the car.

I think I caught every red light between my work and Maddy's. When I got to the store, one of the staff took me to the staff room. She sat in the corner, crying quietly, her head buried in her hands.. One of her co-workers sitting nearby watched as I walked in and went straight to her.

"Maddy?" I whispered, kneeling on the floor in front of her.

She looked up at me, throwing her arms around my neck.

"Mum's in hospital. We need to go. I didn't trust myself to drive like this" she whispered. I hugged her tight.

"Let's go, sweetheart. You can tell me about it in the car," I said.

Maddy clung to my arm the whole way back to the car, unusually quiet. I opened her car door, making sure she was okay before we set off, getting to the hospital as fast as I could without breaking the law.

"Do you know what happened?" I asked. Her knuckles were white from gripping her bag.

"The nurse that called me said she'd had a heart attack. I kept telling her to stop smoking. I knew something like this would happen."

Her breathing was stressed, and I reached for her hand, holding it under mine on the gear lever. The last thing we needed was her stressing over her mother. I glanced at her, and she smiled, and her chest slowed as it rose and fell, presumably reassured by my action.

"They said she was in intensive care," Maddy whispered, as we stood in front of the directory sign at the hospital entrance.

"That's this way, then," I said, squeezing her hand. I didn't know who to be more worried about—Carly or Maddy. If Maddy was getting this wound up, I couldn't even begin to imagine what was going on inside her. It couldn't be good for her or the baby.

Carly lay still, her skin an awful ashen shade I'd never seen on anyone. It was the colour of death, and Maddy let out a sob as she looked at her. There were tubes everywhere, and an oxygen mask over her nose.

"The first forty-eight hours are the most important. If nothing more happens in that time, she stands a better chance of survival. It was a massive heart attack. We'll continue to monitor her, and keep her on oxygen." The doctor spoke softly, reassuringly, and although the news wasn't good, Maddy looked as if the huge weight on her shoulders had been lifted.

I was still worried, though. It was a lot to deal with. Maddy was so close to Carly and if anything happened, I hated to think how she would react.

We could go in to see Carly one at a time, and Maddy obviously went first. She was led to the bedside, and she took her mother's hand, pressing it to her lips. My heart felt like it was breaking into tiny pieces watching them.

I called Damon and told him what had happened.

"Take the time you need," he said, and once again I was so grateful to him. I owed him so much.

For the first time in so long, I sat and prayed for something, anything to happen to get Carly through this. After a while I heard a sound and looked up to see a familiar face.

"Andrew?" he asked.

I stood, nodding. "You're Logan, right?"

"That's right. Sorry for intruding. Bob sent me a text and I just had to come. Is Maddy okay?"

I shrugged. "It's fine. I don't really know how she is. They would only let one of us go in to see Carly, and she's been in there a while."

"Mind if I wait with you? Carly was like a second mother to me."

I nodded. "Sure. Take a seat."

I sat back in the chair, casting my eyes over this guy, the one I'd lost my shit over. He was tall, with dark hair, chin covered in stubble. Dressed in black jeans and a white tank top, his leather jacket flung over his shoulder, he could have walked out of a modelling catalogue. He had a tattoo on his right shoulder that was distracting, and I couldn't help but look at it. It was pretty, all swirls and flames. As if he had the sun on his skin.

I still wasn't sure of him, but if Maddy cared about him that much, he had to be okay.

"I haven't seen either of them for ages. How's Maddy been?"

"Good. She's pregnant. I'm just as worried about her right now as I am Carly."

He nodded, grinning. "Congratulations. Maddy's tough; she'll get through it. She really fucking loves you too. That'll help her."

I cocked an eyebrow at him

Logan laughed. "Don't worry. I kept an eye on her for a long time after we broke up because of all the shit with her father. Once I knew you had her back, I stayed away. She's been a good friend to me—we just weren't right together."

I grinned. "Something works for us."

"And you get to be a dad. That's so cool."

I looked up at the ceiling, worry coursing through my mind. Maddy had to be okay; Carly had to be okay. We all had to leave here together and well and not worry about anything else.

IT MUST HAVE BEEN a good couple of hours before Maddy came back out, heading straight into my arms to cry on my shoulder.

"Hey, what's going on? Are you okay?"

"She's just so still. It's so unlike her and I hate it."

She looked up, turning her head towards Logan. "Hey."

"Hey yourself. Bob let me know what happened. Andrew let me stay here and wait with him."

"Thanks for coming." I thought she might pull away from me, give her old friend a hug to welcome him, but she hung on around my neck, nestling into me.

I helped her to a seat, we sat together and I closed my eyes, resting my hand on her belly. She didn't have much of a bump, but enough that we both knew it was there.

"I'm scared," she whispered.

"I know, but whatever happens we'll deal with it together. We don't have to move; we can stay where we are and look after Carly. We can do whatever you want."

She raised her head, meeting my gaze. I saw fear in her eyes, and I kissed her softly.

Out of the corner of my eye, I saw Logan stand and move towards us. He knelt before Maddy, placing his hands on her knees.

"Maddy, you need to take care of yourself, too. Any time you need to take a break or go home and rest, I'll keep an eye on your mother. I'm not going anywhere until I know what's going on with Carly."

Maddy's chest rose and fell faster and faster as she let out a sob, letting go of me long enough to throw her arms around Logan's neck. He kissed her cheek before she let go and reattached herself to me. Any other time I might have felt a twinge of jealousy. But not now. Not with what was going on.

"You need to listen to Logan and not let the weight of this hang on you, baby," I whispered. "Between the three of us, we got this."

"I should have brought Bob with me. He'll be out of his mind," Logan said.

Maddy nodded. "Can you go and get him?"

"Anything you want, sweetheart."

Logan stood, turning towards the door. "I'll go get us some supplies too. Food and drinks to keep the pregnant lady healthy."

Maddy let out a choked laugh. "He told you already?"

"Yeah, that man of yours is proud of you. It's written all over his face."

I grinned as Maddy turned her face to me, pressing her nose against mine. When we looked up, Logan was gone and it was just the two of us, waiting. Waiting.

TWENTY-SIX

THE HOURS WENT BY. Logan and Bob had returned, but Maddy had already disappeared back in with her mother. I hated that I couldn't sit and hold her hand, but Carly's care was paramount.

A gentle snoring sound from the corner told Logan and I that Bob was asleep.

"Lucky bastard." Logan laughed. "Doubt I'll get much sleep for a while."

"You were really close. To Carly."

He nodded. "Maddy and I went through school together. She was the first girlfriend I ever had. I loved that girl."

"I'm glad she had you. Her father is such a shithead."

Logan laughed. "Have you had a run in with him, then?"

"Yep. He ended up out cold on the floor. He hit her. She's a grown woman and he hit her when she told him she had no money. I thought I'd lost her. She stopped breathing. I have never been so glad to know CPR in all my life."

Logan's expression told me he had no idea about that one, his jaw dropping. "Man, I had no idea."

"I knew I couldn't live without her. My first wife died of an asthma attack. I couldn't do anything to save her. But I saved Maddy, and I'll always be there for her."

He nodded, his dark eyes full of emotion. "I'm glad she met the right one. I certainly wasn't it."

"How long did you two go out for?"

He shrugged. "Three or four years. It was crazy. We were too young, had no idea what we were doing, and probably should never have been together in the first place. After we dated for a while, I decided she'd be the first girl I was ever with. Turned out she didn't want to wait and found someone else to be her first. I found that out after the fact. Loved her so much, we stayed together anyway. Pretty much destined for disaster."

I nodded, and he clasped his hands together as if praying. "We just drifted apart. Not our friendship, that stayed, but the boyfriend-girlfriend thing, we weren't so good at. So we called it quits before we screwed the friendship too."

We both looked towards the room, where Maddy sat beside the bed.

"I never stood a chance," I said. "She knew what she wanted and she went for it. Not that I resisted. What's not to love, right?"

AT THE TWENTY-FOUR HOUR MARK, we convinced Maddy to come home with me for some sleep. Logan and Bob took turns sitting with Carly while we went back to the boarding house, settling in for a rest in Maddy's room.

Despite insisting that she just wouldn't be able to sleep, Maddy was out for the count almost as soon as her head hit the pillow. I lay beside her, my arm under her neck, my hand playing through her hair as I held her close.

When she rolled onto her side, I rolled with her into a spooning position. I rested my hand on her belly.

"Rest easy, my babies," I whispered. Both of them needed the sleep. So did I, and I drifted off to sleep, snuggled up with my wife.

An intense stabbing pain in the arm woke me, and for a moment I wondered if I was having a heart attack. Opening my eyes, I saw Maddy, poking my bare arm with the nail of her index finger, like a damn talon.

"W ... What's happened?" I stammered, forcing my eyes open.

"Nothing. We just slept for ages and I want to go back to the hospital."

I focused my eyes, turning my head to look at the alarm clock.

"About six hours. I guess that's enough."

"Enough?" She began to breathe faster and faster.

"Maddy, calm down. You'll hyperventilate and that's no good for any of us. Let's just shower and get changed before we go."

She shook her head, frowning.

"Come on. You stand there and I'll wash you. The last thing your mother would want is for you to get stressed about this. Not with the baby on the way."

Her shoulders slumped and she nodded, resigned to my logic.

"You're right. I'm just really worried."

"Have there been any missed calls? Has Logan or Bob tried to phone?"

"No."

"Well, there you go. Let's go and sort ourselves out and then get back to the hospital."

Maddy nodded, tears welling in her eyes. I reached up to stroke her face. "Babe, they'll call if anything happens. You know Carly's in good hands—she couldn't be anywhere better."

She nodded and I climbed out of bed, going to the en suite bathroom and turning on the shower. I met her halfway, and took her hand as we went back in to strip off and get under the water.

I washed her down, scrubbing her back while she stood there under the water. All I could do was hope I eased the tension. Carly was the only family she had, other than me, and to lose her would be devastating.

Wrapping a towel around her, I led Maddy back to the bedroom and she let me dry her off. She stood in the centre of the room, naked and forlorn.

"Come on," I said, handing her underwear and then slipping her shirt and skirt on over the top. I wrapped my arms around her, and she relaxed into my chest.

"I could go to sleep again," she said.

"We can if you want to."

Maddy shook her head. "I want to see Mum."

"I know, baby. Let's get going. But you tell me if you need to rest again. I'll be keeping an eye on you."

She looked up at me with the faintest of smiles. "You always do."

"Someone has to," I said, matching her smile. She beamed.

"I'm glad it's you," she whispered.

TWENTY-SEVEN

AFTER FORTY-EIGHT HOURS, Maddy breathed a sigh of relief. This was, of course the safe zone the doctors had spoke about, but from what I could see, Carly looked no better.

We'd managed to catch a few more hours' sleep between the four of us, but we were all exhausted, not wanting to leave Carly alone for any time.

"Maddy, you need more rest," I said. I was worried about her, too. She had large purple bags under her eyes, despite the sleep she'd grabbed.

"I'm fine." It made me so mad that she was that stubborn, but I understood.

This was our third day in the hospital, and as she went to take a shift beside the bed, switching places with Logan, alarms began to go off, the sound of the medical equipment wailing as the doctors and nurses came running to Carly's room.

"No," Maddy whispered. She lurched forward, and I grabbed her, holding her back as she struggled against me.

"They have to do their job," I said.

All we could do was watch, waiting outside the window as they tried their best to save her. First CPR, then the defibrillator—none of it seemed to work, the staff were frantic, raising their voices to call to each other. Maddy buried her face in my chest, and I wrapped my arm around her head to cover her ears. She shook as I held her close to me and when I looked up, the blinds were down as they continued to work on Carly.

"I'm scared," Maddy said.

"Me too, babe. Let's just sit down and wait for the doctor."

She nodded. The truth was, I wanted to keep her off her feet. If I was exhausted, so was she.

We held each other up as we waited, Logan and Bob both sitting opposite us in silence. Waiting, waiting.

After what seemed like an eternity, the door opened, and the doctor walked out. He looked as tired as we were, but the blank look on his face wasn't due to exhaustion, I knew that much.

Maddy jumped to her feet, her face filled with yearning. She appeared unable to see what I saw. Where I saw death, she saw hope.

"I'm so sorry," was all I heard from his mouth. He said so many other things, but none of it meant anything. I held Maddy up until I couldn't, helping her back into a chair and sitting beside her, our arms around each other as I comforted her.

Carly had had another heart attack and her body, already weakened by the first, just hadn't coped. They'd worked on her for some time before deciding it was the end.

They let us in shortly afterward, and all of us gathered around the bed. Maddy was still in my arms, unable to cope with the situation and barely able to look at her mother. The hospital staff had cleared the tubes and machinery away. It was just Carly, asleep and at peace.

Slowly, Maddy reached out to touch her mother's arm, letting out a sob. My heart broke for my wife, losing the person she loved most in the world apart from me. I knew what it was like to lose someone that close.

In the silence of the hospital room, I ached for her. I'd spend my whole life loving and cherishing her to try to fill the gap. My hand rested on the small bump in her belly, and I prayed this would give her the strength to keep going.

BY THE TIME I finally got Maddy out of the hospital, she fell asleep in the car. It was early evening; the darkness had descended enough for the streetlights to be on, and I took a glimpse of her as we travelled the road home again.

Logan and Bob were in the car behind us, and I was glad Logan had been there to take care of Bob. He was as distraught as Maddy. Carly had always been there for him, made sure he was okay, cared for him when no one else would.

The silence was comforting, but unbearable. I wanted to hear Maddy's laughter, her cheery voice which lightened even the darkest night. Her irrepressible love for life had been dulled by the tragedy of the day.

She woke as we pulled up at the house, Logan swinging in behind us, and I went around the car and opened the door to help her out.

"I feel like I could sleep for a week," she murmured.

"Then you should do. Everything else can wait." I kissed her head, slipping my arm around her waist as I helped her inside.

We didn't bother going up to my room, and opened up the rooms she had shared with her mother for so long, inviting Logan and Bob in to sit on the couch and have coffee with us.

Maddy lasted about five minutes before she left to go to bed, and the three of us sat with that awful silence for a while before Bob sighed.

"I don't know what I'm going to do now," he said. "What's going to happen to this place?"

I shrugged. "I'm not sure. We'll have to find out what Carly's will says, I guess, and take it from there."

Logan patted Bob on the back. "You can always come and work with me at the workshop. I could do with some help at times."

"Thanks, Logan. We'll see."

I smiled at him,

Logan held up his cup of coffee. "This would be so much better if it was a beer."

I laughed. "If I had any, I'd get us all one."

"This will have to do then. Cheers," he said, raising his cup.

"For Carly," I said, clinking mine with his. Bob grinned, and did the same. "Now, we just have to take care of Maddy, make sure she's going to be okay."

Logan nodded. "She's stronger than she looks. It's a blow, but if anyone can get through this, it'll be Maddy."

I took a sip of my coffee. He was right, but my biggest concern was the baby. Maddy was strong, but in a vulnerable state right now.

Maybe I needed to find her a distraction.

TWENTY-EIGHT

I FOUND A DISTRACTION FOR MADDY. Looking for houses. It took us three months to find the perfect one, and she found a real bargain. The woman who owned it had been in some financial strife, left by a husband who had walked out on her and their children. My heart went out to her, and my guilt at finding such a bargain was tempered by the love I had for my own family. What it must be like for her starting again.

Carly had left the boarding house to Maddy, and she'd decided to put Bob in charge of the place. He'd learned a lot over the years with Carly and he had me to help him out with the business side of things. Rather than taking more people in, he'd run it as it was until they all moved out—no one ever stayed that long—then we'd re-evaluate how things were. It would buy us a few months to worry about it at least, and keep a roof over Bob's head.

The new house itself wasn't much to look at. It was clean and tidy, inside and out. The garden was a little overgrown, but nothing I couldn't take care of, with plenty of space to plant flowers for Maddy, and for our child to play.

For us, it was paradise and for the first time since Carly's death, Maddy's smile was genuine.

"This is for us?" she whispered, cuddling up to me. We stood at the front gate, looking at our new home.

"If you want it. Things will be tight for a while, but we can do it, Maddy."

I placed my hand on her belly, just as our baby kicked. "Yes, little one, you too."

Maddy rolled her eyes. "I swear, the way this baby moves, it's like a monkey swinging in a tree."

"Hello, little monkey," I said, patting the bump.

She grinned, placing her hand over mine and leaning into me. My heart swelled at the thought of providing this home for them. My family.

There was a time I never thought I'd get to say those words.

We moved in before the month was out. Maddy was excited and couldn't wait to get stuck into making the place ours.

Maddy was six months pregnant now, and blooming.

The outspoken, pushy, often scantily-clad young woman I'd fallen in love with had undergone a transformation during her pregnancy. She became more mature, thoughtful, such a sweet delight whose passion for me burned hotter than the sun in the middle of summer, drawing me in deeper than I thought possible.

This house was the icing on the cake.

On the first day, I'd moved the living room furniture around three times before she was happy. We didn't even make it to the other rooms. She stood, one arm folded over the other, holding a finger to her mouth while she took in our surroundings.

"You know, it is going to take all day just to get one room sorted if we do this," I said.

"Are you complaining?" she asked, grinning.

"Yes." I sat on the couch, crossing my arms as if refusing to do anything else.

She moved towards me, and I grabbed her, pulling her onto my lap and laughing as she landed awkwardly on top of me.

"Be careful." She pouted.

"I'm always careful." I laid my hand on her belly, gently stroking her and our baby. My two favourite things.

"Am I being a pain in the butt?" she asked, her dark eyes seeking the answer in mine.

"Truthfully? Yes."

She laughed, slapping my arm.

"I'm still glad you're mine," I said, raising my hand to her cheek and pulling her down for a kiss.

"Good, 'cause you're stuck with me." Maddy grinned, wrapping her arms around my neck.

It wasn't possible to be any happier.

By the end of the first weekend we were settled in. Everything was where we wanted it to be—the only thing left was the baby's room.

Maddy freaked out when I brought in one more box, one she didn't know about, one I placed in the room we'd decided was for our child.

"What's that?"

"You'll see."

Tears streamed down her cheeks as I tore open the cardboard. and started assembling the cot. This made it all real. Our home—our baby—our new life.

"Andrew," she whispered.

I stood. The cot was half assembled, one end and the base connected, but she was more important. I took her in my arms, holding her close.

"It's okay," I said. I closed my eyes as she cried on my shoulder.

"I love it." She raised her head, her eyes still full of tears.

"Let me finish putting it together. There's a mattress in the box, we just need to get sheets and stuff, but I figured you would want to do that."

She nodded, still clinging to me.

"I love you, Maddy. More than anything. I want to give you and our baby everything."

"You already have," she whispered.

TWENTY-NINE

THE LAST TRIMESTER of Maddy's pregnancy passed slowly. We had our new house to keep us busy, but she was well over it by the seven-month mark and couldn't wait for the baby to be born.

Trailing kisses down her body, I looked twice at her navel before laughing.

"What's this?"

Maddy giggled. "I got my belly button pierced."

I cocked at eyebrow. "Are you supposed to do that when you're pregnant?"

She sighed. "I have no idea, but I did it anyway. I thought it looked cool."

In typical Maddy style, she was finding ways to keep herself entertained and occupied until the baby arrived. If a piercing kept her happy, it was pretty minor.

I stroked the stud. She usually had an innie, but in the advanced stages of pregnancy, it had turned into an outie. "So what happens when your belly button goes back to normal?"

"I don't know. Can you just get on with what you were doing before you noticed it?"

I rolled my eyes, shaking my head. Our already highly-sexed relationship had gone into overdrive the closer Maddy got to giving birth. Now we were mere weeks from our big day, and she couldn't get enough of me. Luckily, I couldn't get enough of her either. I didn't think it was possible for us to be in any better position for the birth of our child—madly in love, and waiting for the big day.

I followed the curve of her belly with my tongue, and she sighed loudly as I began to play her. I could make her body sing, and I closed my eyes as I lost myself in this beautiful woman. My beautiful woman.

I rolled over, reaching for Maddy and finding the bed still warm, but empty. She'd been having trouble sleeping as her baby bump grew, making lying down more uncomfortable as she tried to find the perfect position that wouldn't make her back ache.

My eyelids still heavy, I lay back and waited for her to return. I loved waking up with her, but that would be disrupted for a while, at least until the baby came.

And then I heard her, the shrill shriek of her disagreeing with someone. I sighed, sliding out of bed, and moving towards the noise. Maddy never let anyone win an argument, and I cringed at us falling out with the neighbours already.

"I don't know," she yelled. Her hands were formed into fists, her face red from how upset she was.

Some guy was standing at the door with an equally red face. I had about a foot on him, so I hoped that would cause him to back off. Whatever was going on, I did not like my pregnant wife having to deal with it.

"What the hell is going on?" I said. Maddy spun towards me, her nostrils flaring as I stopped her in full noise. I almost pitied the guy on the doorstep, but he'd clearly got her into this state.

"This guy is looking for the people that used to live here, and he won't believe me when I say I don't know where they are."

I moved towards her, gathering her into my arms. She shook as she slipped her arms around my waist.

"You think yelling at a pregnant woman is really a good idea? I don't give a crap why you're here. Get off my property or I'll call the police."

His expression darkened, but I towered over him, moving Maddy behind me.

"My family used to live here. My wife and children."

"Well, they don't live here now."

I took a step back, closing the door in his face and turning towards Maddy. She buried her face in my chest, tears rolling down my bare skin.

"He just wouldn't go," she whispered.

"If what the real estate agent said was true, he doesn't deserve to find his family." I eased away from her, tilting her face towards me with my finger under her chin. "I'd never do that to you, Maddy. Even if things ever turned to crap between us, I would hope we could work things out. I'm telling you now, I'd never turn my back on you."

"I love you so much," she whispered.

I bent my head, kissing her on the nose. "I love you too. Now, come back to bed and get warm. I could do with some more sleep, with you beside me."

She gazed up at me, a defiant look in her eye. "I'm going to find that lady that used to live here and be her friend. She'll need as many friends as she can get with an asshole of a husband like that."

I laughed, pulling her by the hand back towards the bedroom. If I knew anything about Maddy, it was that she'd follow through. That poor woman wouldn't know what had hit her.

The following week turned out to be the most peaceful in a long time. Maddy still worked during the day, but instead of moping around in the evenings, complaining that she wanted her pregnancy to come to an end, she found another hobby. Amateur detective.

Determined to track down the woman who had sold us the house, Maddy put all her efforts into finding where she'd got to, and by the end of the week she was triumphant.

I came home to find her on the phone, laughing with someone.

"Thanks, Logan," she said as she hung up.

"How is he?" I asked.

"Great. You will never guess what he just told me." She grabbed my hand, pulling me down onto the couch. I leaned over and kissed her.

"What?"

"Remember last weekend? That awful man that showed up here?"

I nodded. How could I forget? She'd only been talking about it for the past week.

"I found his wife. She was right under my nose. Well, Logan's nose."

I rubbed my forehead. "Sorry, you've lost me. Where is she?"

She sat back, raising her eyebrows and looking smug. "She moved into the same apartment block he lives in." Maddy tilted her head. "He says she's hot."

I laughed. "Those are Logan's words, I presume."

Her eyes widened. "He said her ex turned up. Logan was so glad to be there. The guy went to hit her, but Logan stopped him."

"Holy shit."

"Yeah. Logan said the guy nearly crapped himself and got out of there pretty fast."

She wrapped her arms around my waist, cuddling in tight. I closed my eyes, hugging her back. "I'm so glad I have you," she whispered.

"I don't know how anyone could ever hurt anyone that was so precious to them. All I ever want to do is wrap you up in cotton wool."

Maddy laughed, kissing me on the cheek.

I rubbed her back. "I mean it, Maddy—nothing in this world is ever going to hurt you if I can help it."

After dinner, she'd given in to the call of bed and gone for an early night.

I stayed behind, washing the dishes before settling on the couch in front of the television. Soon enough, my eyelids were heavy, and I leaned back into the cushions with a yawn. I might have gotten up and gone to bed if I could have been bothered standing.

The phone ringing made me jump, and I grabbed it from the cradle, juggling it before managing to get a hold and answering.

"Hello?"

"Andrew, I'm glad it's you. It's Bob."

I smiled. He had hit his stride looking after the boarding house, and Maddy had agreed to him staying there long-term, as long as he took care of it and kept it running like her mother had. I don't think he had any intention of letting either Maddy or Carly down.

"Hey, Bob. How's it going?"

"Maddy's dad called."

I sat up, gripping the phone.

"What did he want?"

"It took him a while. He'd just heard about Carly. Wanted to find out what was happening with the house and where Maddy was."

I gulped. "You didn't tell him where Maddy was, did you?"

"Hell no. Kid's like a daughter to me. I just wanted to let you know he might be looking for her."

I closed my eyes. After everything, now was not the time for this. As if Maddy needed anything else to worry about.

"He's in prison. Doing time for an armed robbery. He'll be in for a while, but I still thought I should tell you."

"Thanks, Bob," I said, relieved at least that he couldn't get to Maddy any time soon.

It might just be time to pay him a visit.

THIRTY

THE PRISON HADN'T CHANGED; not that I'd expected it to. I'd called ahead to make sure Russell Jones would see me, and I guess he was as curious about me as I was about him.

I hoped that now that he was locked away, the news that his wife was dead was eating him alive. *All the shitty things he'd done to her ... and to Maddy.*

I'd vowed never to come back here, and right now, looking at the building, bile rose in my throat at the thought of going inside. Maybe I was a visitor this time, but the memory of being trapped, unable to go anywhere, punched me in the gut. It would have been so easy to walk away.

My knuckles were white on the steering wheel. The last time I'd felt like this was when I'd returned to the park, sitting in the car after seeing Rowan and Kyle. Nerves ate away at me. I checked the time. 9.57 am. I had to face him.

I paused before the front office door, taking a deep breath before pulling at the handle. It was now or never. *For Maddy.*

As I signed in the visitor book, a guard appeared from out the back and smiled at me, cocking his head in recognition.

"I know you."

"Yeah," I said. "I lived here for three years."

He laughed. "That's right. I like to think I have a good memory. What are you doing back?"

"Visiting my father-in-law."

He gaped and I grinned, gaining confidence by the second. Despite the memories of this place washing over me, I had nothing to fear this time.

When he came into the room, I felt a rush of adrenalin, . It was as if iced water raced down my spine, as if a primal urge threatened to grip me. Last time I saw him, I'd knocked him out. I'd never met him formally.

"You're Andrew. Maddy's friend," he said as he sat down.

"I'm her husband."

He raised an eyebrow at that. Obviously he hadn't heard about his daughter's marriage.

"Husband, huh?"

"Yeah. Bob called and told me that you were trying to get hold of Maddy."

He looked at the table, dropping the eye contact. "I heard about Carly. Wanted to make sure my little girl was okay."

The anger built again. His little girl? As if he gave a crap.

"She's fine. Better than fine."

He looked back up and I met his eyes, so like Maddy. His hair was dark, graying at the sides, and he had slight stubble on the chin that he was now scratching at nervously.

"I don't want you contacting her. I don't want you seeing her. She doesn't need any more stress right now. She's coping with her mother's death and she's pregnant."

He looked up, and I could swear I saw a glint of emotion in his eye. "She's having a baby?"

"Yes. I'm here to tell you to stay away. If I had any say I'd make them leave you locked up in here. But one day you'll get out, and I don't want you part of her life."

Memories of Kyle warning me to stay away from Rowan echoed in my ears. That day in the park, when I'd finally snapped and went straight to their place and committed my crime. I understood Kyle's actions more than ever now.

Russell sat in silence, staring back at me, and his eyes were pained as if I had hurt him. But he'd hurt Maddy more, and for that I would never forgive this man I didn't even know.

Her scar was a constant reminder of what he'd done.

The relief of stepping back out of that building was immeasurable, and I stood beside the car, leaning on it for support and taking huge gulps of breath. I'd never take my freedom for granted. Ever.

Logan's car was in the driveway when I got home and Maddy shrieked as I walked in the door. I loosened my tie; I was ready for a stiff drink.

"Andrew, look at what Logan bought us."

In the centre of the living room was a rocking chair, perfect for Maddy to sit on and nurse the baby.

"Bought you, you mean. Where's my present?" I grinned at Logan, who shook his head and laughed.

"I figure the less stressed she gets, the less stress you get," he said, reaching up to shake my hand.

I took his hand in mine and Maddy kissed me on the cheek before disappearing with promises of a drink.

"How's it going?" he asked.

"I saw Maddy's father today," I said, keeping my voice low so she didn't hear me.

"No shit. How did that go?"

"He called Bob to get in contact with Maddy. Wanted to say how sorry he was about Carly. I went and told him to leave her the hell alone."

Logan raised an eyebrow and nodded. "Good move. She doesn't need that shit. Now she's got you, she doesn't need to worry about it any more."

I leaned back on the couch, lifting my feet and resting them on the coffee table. Maddy would tell me off, but I was too tired to care.

"How are things going with you? I heard you have a hot neighbour."

Logan shook his head, looking down and grinning as if he had some big secret. "Olivia's amazing. She's got these two awesome kids, and she just works so hard. I don't want to push her; she's been through a lot, but I'm kind of hoping things go my way."

"Good for you. Gotta grab happiness where you can. I can tell you now that her ex was a real douchebag. I don't even know the guy and I can say that."

"I already told her I think he's an idiot. Who walks away from the perfect woman?"

Maddy returned with a bourbon and cola and leaned over the back of the couch to kiss me.

"How did you know I needed this?" I asked.

"I know you better than anybody," she said, her eyes full of desire, something even Logan didn't miss.

"Uh, guys, I think I'll get out of here and let you enjoy your evening." He smirked as he stood, grabbing my hand to shake again.

Maddy lifted her chin at him. "Later."

She turned back to me. "Now, where were we?"

THIRTY-ONE

THE BIRTH of our daughter changed my life.

All of a sudden, I had a bundle with all this blonde fluff on her head in my arms, and I fell head over heels. She looked up at me with her big blue eyes, and I felt the pull of being her father. She was just as beautiful as her mother, and made just as much noise. Seriously, that kid had the biggest set of lungs, and I had no idea how she stored them in that tiny body.

We were both so in love we decided we wanted a houseful of children. Well, maybe three.

"What are we going to call her?" Maddy asked. We'd decided that we'd wait until we saw her to name her, and now I had no idea.

"You can name her whatever you like. I don't care, she's Daddy's Little Girl to me," I said, cradling our daughter, stroking the blonde fluff.

"Well, aren't you just useless? Maybe I should name her Moonbeam, or Sunshine. She looks like a Sunshine."

I held my daughter's little feet in my hands, marvelling that they could both fit inside my fist. She really was precious.

"Whatever you want," I said, completely distracted.

"Andrew, I thought we could call her Carly."

I looked up at Maddy. She looked sad, as if she wanted to cry. "Maddy, I think it's a beautiful name. And you're beautiful, and this little one is beautiful." I shifted my focus back to the baby, who had wriggled free of my useless swaddling. "I think Carly is a perfect."

With my free hand, I reached for Maddy, and she smiled.

My rainbow.

MADDY and I were both soon exhausted, and loving every second of it. But Carly's birth also brought nightmares over what I'd done to Rowan, and how I'd separated her from her baby, back to the forefront of my mind. When I wasn't waking with Maddy as she fed Carly in the night, I was waking myself, shaking as I relived Rowan begging me to let her go to her child.

I would have given anything to be able to throw myself at her mercy, beg her forgiveness, but I had already apologised and contacting her again was out of the question. There was only one thing I could do—take care of my family the best I could.

Maddy didn't even notice; she had her own exhaustion to take care of. Carly was a feeding, pooping machine and I did my best to help Maddy, but we were both so damn tired.

"Sleep when the baby sleeps," she said. "What happens when the baby doesn't sleep?"

I shrugged. After the birth, I'd taken a couple of weeks off work to be with my family, but now I was back on the job and almost sleeping through work. Something had to get better. Anything.

And then, like an angel, my mother arrived, and did all those things Carly would have done for Maddy. She had that magic touch with the baby and we finally managed to get some shut-eye.

Not only did I admire Maddy for what she'd gone through, but also I had a whole new appreciation for Mum.

We were finally back on track.

THIRTY-TWO

Three years later ...

LIFE WAS NOT all roses with us, not by a long shot.

Maddy was pregnant for the second time. This time we'd planned it, waiting for Carly to be a little older before trying for another baby, and it was hitting Maddy much harder.

Her mood swings were more prominent, and I never knew what I was going to encounter coming home from work each day. Carly never saw it. Maddy was consistent in her attitude toward her, but I was the one she took everything out on.

I understood. A lot of it was her missing her mother more than ever. Getting through Carly's birth and the early days had been hard. Logan would come and see her sometimes, always planning his visits when he knew I'd be home to avoid any misunderstanding. He had a family of his own now, so visits were few and far between. Most of the time, it was just the two of us.

Maddy was often exhausted, but resistant to sending Carly to day-care, even for part of the day. I backed off and left her to it, working out a way to bring work home so I could support her if she needed me.

By the time she got to ten weeks, she was on edge and resisting going back to the doctor, confident it was just a matter of time before she felt better. It drove me nuts, but I'd learned a long time ago not to try to force her hand, not unless she was in danger.

I should have done it anyway.

It was Friday night, and the end of a long week for me. Work was busier than ever, and my head was throbbing with everyone making demands.

"Daddy, I'm hungry," Carly whined, five minutes after I'd arrived home.

"I'm just going to make us some dinner, sweetheart. You snuggle up with Mum on the couch, and I'll bring you something shortly."

I rested my hand on Maddy's shoulder. "Do you want anything in particular? If Carly's already hungry, I might just cook scrambled eggs and bacon."

"Whatever," she grumbled.

Taking a deep breath, I headed to the kitchen. Small footsteps told me Carly had followed.

"Mummy's tired."

I bent, tapping her on the nose. "I know, sweetie. We have to take really good care of her."

"She's grumpy."

I opened my arms, hugging her as she came closer. "It's okay, Carly. She'll be happier soon. She's just feeling a bit yucky at the moment."

She nodded. "Can I have chicken nuggets?" Her favourite food, and my running joke with Maddy, as when Carly had them for dinner she always seemed happier and slept better, leaving us more time alone.

I laughed. "I'm going to cook eggs. They cook much faster. I know you like those too."

"Eggs are from chickens."

"That's right. So not unlike a chicken nugget." I knew I was stretching it; I just hoped that I'd gotten my three-year-old logic right.

"Okay," she said. She pulled away from me, skipping back to the living room and her mother.

Dinner didn't take long to cook at all, and the aroma of grilled bacon filled the house, smelling delicious.

I carried out two plates of scrambled eggs on toast and bacon for my girls. Carly clapped excitedly as I placed one down in front of her. Maddy clapped her hand across her mouth, moaning as she ran for the bathroom.

"Mummy's sick," Carly said. She hadn't even bothered with the fork I'd put on her plate, her small hand was wrapped around a slice of streaky bacon.

"Yes, she is." I sighed. Poor Maddy couldn't cut a break.

I followed her to the bathroom. She was leaned over the toilet, and with nothing in her stomach, wasn't getting anywhere.

"Can I get you anything to help?" I asked.

"The smell of that food made me want to hurl," she said. "Not that there's anything wrong with your cooking."

"I'm glad of that, at least." I ran my fingers through her hair, pulling it back off her face and into a ponytail in one hand. She was warm, and I put my hand to her neck to feel just how warm she was.

Fishing for the ear thermometer in the top drawer, I finally found it, gently inserting it in her ear just as she retched.

"What the hell are you doing?" She grumped, pulling away from me as it beeped.

"You're warm. I'm just checking to see if you're okay." I studied the piece of metal. Her temperature was up slightly, but nothing too worrying. "I think you're okay." I reached back into the drawer for a hair elastic, tying her hair up off her face.

"I'm so awful and you are so good to me." Maddy reached up, stroking my hand.

"No, you're just pregnant and having a shitty time of it. It'll get better. Do you want anything else?"

Her smile paled in brilliance against any one of the beautiful grins she'd ever given me.

"No. I'm just going to sit here for a minute and then I'll come back out. Can you get rid of the plate and let me know when Carly's finished?"

"You know by the time I'm back out there, Carly will have eaten your bacon too."

Maddy laughed. "I bet anything you're right."

SHE'D SMILED through the rest of the evening, fooling Carly that everything was okay right up until bedtime.

Carly had gone to sleep without complaint as she usually did, and I went back out to the living room where Maddy sat, still and miserable.

"How are you really feeling?" I asked.

She shrugged. "Like crap. Really uncomfortable and crampy."

"Do you think we should get you looked at by a doctor?"

She stood. "I think I really want a good night's sleep."

"Come on then." I stood beside her, placing my palm on her cheek.

"Oh, stop it, Andrew. Stop fussing. I'll be fine."

"I'm allowed to fuss. You're my wife and that's my baby you're carrying. Whatever it takes to make you feel better."

She pulled away, turning towards the bedroom.

"Just leave me alone. I'll get some sleep and maybe I'll be better in the morning."

I sighed, and turned to sit back on the couch, knowing I couldn't win.

"I'm sorry if I make you unhappy." Her words pierced my heart. That was the opposite of how I felt.

"You make me very happy; you have no idea how much you changed my life."

"The only reason you married me was because I was pregnant," she shrieked, and we both just stood there in stunned silence, the words hanging heavy in the air.

"That's not true." I took a step towards her, looking for something in her eyes, anything that told me she had just said it, not believed it.

"Of course it is, Andrew." She sounded resigned, tired, over it all.

"Maddy, if you think for one minute that is the only reason we stayed together, you are so wrong. This whole being-sick thing is overwhelming. We need to see a doctor tomorrow. It's just too much."

Tears streamed down her face, her arms flat against her side in resignation. "I bullied you into this, pushed you into having a relationship with me. You're in love with your dead wife, and I just remind you of her sometimes. I'm not stupid."

In an instant, I had her in my arms, my lips on hers, hoping against hope that my need for her would translate in my kiss. Surely she could see if I hadn't wanted to be with her, I would never have wanted the baby that now grew inside her, let alone Carly. They were my life, everything to me, and I needed her to understand that.

There was pressure on my chest from the palms of her hands as she tried to push me away, but I wasn't about to let go of her now. This had clearly been building for a long time, and was so far from the truth.

"Don't fight me," I whispered. "I love you, Maddy, whatever you think. You and Carly are everything to me, and I'm not just with you because of her. I'm with you because I love you." She relaxed and the pressure against my ribs eased as I stroked her hair. "Why don't we go to bed and get some sleep? You've been so tired and cranky with this pregnancy, and I want to pamper you, make you feel better."

Her body went limp as she surrendered, and I let her go, taking her hand in mine and leading her into the bedroom.

"I'm sorry," she whispered, "I feel so awful all the time right now, and you are the last person I should be taking it out on. I didn't mean it. Any of it."

She put her arms up as I lifted her T-shirt over her head, just like I did when helping Carly get into her pyjamas.

"That's what I'm here for. You can yell and scream at me as much as you like, but I'm going nowhere. I'm right where I want to be."

I slid her nightgown over her head, pulling her leggings down as it fell over her legs.

"Get into bed. Want a back rub?"

She nodded, leaning against my chest, slipping her arms around my waist. "You're so good to me and I'm just being a bitch to you."

"If I was worried about that, I never would have married you." She raised her face to look at me, one eyebrow raised, and I grinned back at her. "You're stuck with me, baby. Always."

She lifted her nose in the air. "I guess I can live with that."

"Now, get in bed and I'll go and make you a hot chocolate. That should help you sleep. Then back rub, cuddle, and sleep."

Maddy climbed into bed, screwing up her face at me. She formed a circle with her thumb and index finger, poking through it with her other index finger. "Don't you want to do this?"

I laughed all the way out to the kitchen. Maybe we were having a rocky time, but the love was there and just as strong as it had been all this time.

We had to find our way back to it.

SHE WAS SITTING up in bed when I got back, fighting the urge to sleep, her head nodding as her eyelids dropped, then springing back open as she looked up again.

"Get this down you and we'll get some rest. Gotta look after my girl."

Running her finger around the rim of the mug, she stared into it. "I wouldn't blame you if you didn't want me as your girl."

I slipped between the sheets, and reached up to stroke her arm. "You'll always be my girl, Maddy. None of this shit matters. We can argue to the moon and back and I'll be here. You don't have any reason to be insecure or doubt me. Since the day I saw you on those stairs, all I've ever seen is you."

Her eyes were full of sadness as she turned her head to look at me. "I'm still sorry."

"You have nothing to be sorry about. We promised to stick together through good times and bad. That's all that matters."

Every sip she took, her eyes closed just that little bit more and I took the mug from her when she'd drained the cup.

"Can I get a rain check on that back rub?" she asked.

She rested her head on the pillow as I nodded. I smiled, sliding my arm over her. "Sleep well, sweetheart."

I watched as she fell asleep, her expression finally peaceful as she got the rest she needed. Her pregnancy with Carly had been so carefree; this one had been trouble from day one. I could only hope it would get better.

THIRTY-THREE

"ANDREW."

I stirred, her hands pushing at my arm to wake me. The faint light from the bedside lamp illuminated the room enough for me to see her leaning over me, her face crossed with worry.

"What is it?" I pushed myself up into a seating position.

"Something's wrong. I've got this really sharp pain and I'm bleeding." She was pale, tears staining her cheeks, and I wondered how long she'd put up with it before waking me.

"Okay." I was already out of bed before I finished the word, pulling on a shirt and grabbing some pants.

"What are you doing?"

"We're getting you to the hospital."

She just sat there, looking up at me.

"Come on, sweetheart. Let's get your bathrobe on and get out of here," I said, stroking her face with my finger.

"But Carly ..."

"Carly will just have to come with us. I'll grab her and get her in the car. Take your time and I'll come back."

Maddy nodded, grabbing hold of my hand. "I'm scared," she

whispered. My heart was racing, but I couldn't show her just how terrified I was. I had to be calm.

"Me too. So let's get you somewhere you can be taken care of."

My baby girl was dreaming when I went to get her, and she sank her head onto my shoulder as soon as I picked her up, still sleeping.

"Sorry, Carly. We gotta go for a drive now," I whispered.

I grabbed the fleecy blanket from her bed, snuggling it around her while I carried her out to the garage, leaving the door open to the house so Maddy could follow. I strapped Carly into her seat, placing the blanket on top of her. She stirred, looking up before her head fell to rest on the side of her seat. At least she wouldn't be freaking out at her mother's discomfort.

I ran back to the bedroom, entering just as Maddy clutched at her stomach. She doubled over as she leaned on the bed.

"Hey," I whispered, placing a hand on her back. I walked around the bed, picking up my wallet and phone.

"Wait a minute. I just need this to stop hurting and then I can move." She closed her eyes, intense concentration all over her face as she rode it out.

"Want me to carry you to the car?" She looked up at me, shaking her head, but her eyes were so full of pain that I ignored her, bending to pick her up.

She stared out of the window as I jumped in the driver's side. "Let's get you to a doctor."

We all sat in silence, apart from Carly's occasional snore. I glanced at Maddy, smiling at the similarities between her and Carly. She looked so serious, more so than I'd seen her in a long time. The past few weeks we'd fought like cat and dog, but whatever happened tonight had stopped that in its tracks.

How long has she been feeling awful?

Her hand landed softly on my arm. "Don't speed. We all want to get there in one piece." Her breathing was laboured, and I just knew she was in more discomfort than she let on.

I wanted to put my foot down, drive as fast as I could. Anything to get her there and under medical care. I held back, because she was right, and because I carried the most precious cargo I ever could.

Carly had woken by the time we got to the hospital, and I parked as close as I could, carrying her as Maddy walked beside me. It felt like an eternity passed between getting out of the car and getting to the hospital door, Maddy was walking so slowly. If I could, I would have carried them both in.

Thankfully, there was a wheelchair just inside the door, and I helped Maddy into it, placing Carly down to walk. If we hadn't been somewhere new and bright, she might have grumbled, but there was far too much to look at as we made the short trip to the accident and emergency department.

A nurse greeted us as we came in and took us straight to a bed, where she and I helped Maddy lie down. Calling for a doctor, she started checking Maddy over while I filled in the paperwork. Carly sat beside me, leaning against my arm.

It took what felt like an age for them to decide to give her an ultrasound, but as soon as they did that, they found the problem.

"Your pregnancy is ectopic. What that means—" the doctor started.

"I know what that means, I'm not stupid," Maddy snapped.

I placed my hand on her arm. "Babe, let the doctor speak. At least if it's confirmed they can deal with it."

She pouted.

"Maddy, I know you're cranky and in pain. They can help."

She nodded, looking up at the doctor. "Sorry."

"It's okay, Mrs Carmichael. We are going to have to perform surgery to avoid anything happening."

"Will I lose the fallopian tube?" she asked.

He sat on the bed at her feet. "I can't answer that until we've taken a look. It might be that the pregnancy is ending itself, given your symptoms tonight."

"All this has just made me so bitchy," she said.

"Bitchier," I said it before I even thought the word, and was relieved when she laughed.

"I'm sorry, Andrew. I knew something wasn't quite right, but didn't know what it was. I just thought this was hitting me harder than with Carly."

I took her hand in mine. "It doesn't matter. What matters is making sure you're well again."

After admitting her, I helped her into a wheelchair and a nurse pushed her down the corridor towards the room where they would prepare her for surgery.

Carly grew heavy in my arms as she fell back to sleep. I was tired, stressed beyond belief, an ache starting in my stomach and spreading to my chest. If I stopped for a moment, I'd fall apart, but I couldn't do that in front of Maddy. She was scared enough for both of us.

Maddy climbed from the wheelchair to the bed, and as much as I loved having my daughter in my arms for reassurance, I wanted to hold my wife.

Sat in a chair beside the bed, I rocked Carly, still fast asleep . As the nurses came and left, and the doctor made arrangements for her surgery, all I could think of was what my life was before Maddy.

She'd given me more than she could ever know. I'd lost one woman I loved, I couldn't do it again.

With no idea how serious this was until they operated, I was a mess of emotion inside.

"I just want you to be safe," I said.

Tears welled in her eyes as she looked at me. "I'm so sorry."

"For what?"

"For everything. I was so awful to you tonight and here you are, holding my hand and loving me, the way you always do."

I squeezed her fingers. "It doesn't matter. You know how much I love you. Nothing's ever going to change that."

She smiled, and I raised her hand to my lips, brushing a kiss across it.

Please be okay.

THIRTY-FOUR

KNOWING NOW we could be here for hours, I needed to work out what to do with Carly. Sleeping in my arms didn't really work for either of us. She needed a bed, a proper sleep, and a distraction while her mother was having surgery.

"I'll call Logan, he'll take her," Maddy said. She fished her phone out of her bag, and sat with it to her ear as she made the call.

"Damn it. Straight to voicemail." She slapped her palm to her forehead. "Oh, he was going away this weekend. I bet they've already gone."

"It's okay. If she has to stay here, she has to stay here."

"We could always leave her with Bob. You know he'll take good care of her."

I grimaced. "As much as I like the guy, I don't like the idea of leaving her in that place, and you know he's not going to want to go anywhere."

Maddy's face fell. "I wish we were closer to your parents. They'd take her in a heartbeat."

"It'll be morning by the time they get here. Unless ..." I shook my head. "No, that would never work."

"What?" She looked at me quizzically.

I stood. Carly stirred in my arms and I kissed her cheek. "I'll be back shortly."

Maddy grabbed my arm. "Where are you going?"

"Somewhere I know she'll be safe. Now rest." I leaned over to kiss her softly. "I'll take care of Carly, and you just get better. I'll try to make it back before your surgery, but if I'm not back in time, I'll be here when you wake up."

She chewed her bottom lip, looking nervously at Carly. "I wish you would tell me what you were doing."

"Going to see a friend. Don't worry about us. And do what you're told. It'll be the first time, but the doctor knows what is best."

She crossed her arms, and frowned. "I'll try."

"Be back soon and I'll tell you all about it."

I leaned over, kissing her on the forehead. "If I don't make it back, I'll be here when you wake up. Promise. I love you, Maddy Carmichael."

"Love you too."

I buckled a sleepy Carly in her car seat, and she grumbled, looking up at me with sleepy eyes. "We're going somewhere you can have a proper sleep, sweetie. Hopefully you can stay there."

Maddy would have gone nuts if she knew where I was going, but there was only one person in this town I would trust with my daughter. Someone who might not want to help me, but would surely help Carly. Rowan.

ALTHOUGH IT WAS LATE, the living room light was on when I pulled up outside. Last time I was here, it was to talk Rowan into leaving with me, and when she said no, I did the most stupid thing I'd ever done.

When I'd said my goodbyes in the park, I'd never planned to see her again. But this was a special case, and I knew Carly would be safe and sound here.

"Come on, baby." I said, unbuckling her harness.

She rubbed her eyes, flopping her head on my shoulder. "I'm tired, Daddy."

"I know."

I took a deep breath, gathering the courage to knock on the door.

"Who's that at this time of night?" I heard Rowan ask.

"I'll get it," Kyle said, his footsteps already coming towards the door. After what happened, I was sure he was ultra protective of her, even after all this time.

The outside light went on, and the door swung open. I'd be the last person he'd expect to see.

He set his jaw at sight of me before narrowing his eyes as he took in Carly on my shoulder. "Andrew?"

Rowan appeared behind him. "What?"

She did the same as him, raising an eyebrow.

"What are you doing here?" Kyle asked.

"I have no right to be here—" I started.

"Damn right you don't," he said. "I'm calling the police."

He turned his head toward Rowan as she placed her hand on his arm, nodding towards Carly.

"Is that your little girl?" she asked.

"I didn't steal her, if that's what you mean." I said the words so harshly, and didn't mean them that way. She recoiled, and Kyle stepped in front of her.

I sighed. "Look, sorry. It's just been a really long day and you two are the only people I can think of who might be able to help me with Carly. I need somewhere for her to sleep, where I can leave her and know she'll be safe."

"Where are you planning to go?" Kyle said. Always suspicious, and rightfully so.

"What's her name? Mum said something about you having a

child." Rowan pushed Kyle aside, moving a little closer to look at my daughter.

"Carly. It was my wife's mother's name."

She smiled. "Oh. I thought you said Charlie for a minute. We have a Charlie, a little boy about her age."

I nodded, smiling, unsure of what to even say to that. "To answer Kyle's question, Maddy has an ectopic pregnancy she has to have surgery for. We've been at the hospital the last hour or so, and she's going into surgery soon. It's no place for Carly, and I don't have anyone to take care of her. I was wondering if she could stay with you for the night."

They looked at each other, Kyle cocking an eyebrow at Rowan. It was unnerving for a moment, as they seemed to communicate without talking. His stance softened.

"You really have no one?" Kyle asked.

I shook my head. "There was Maddy's mother, but she died before Carly was born. It's just been the three of us these past few years. If I have to, Carly can stay at the hospital with me, but it's not going to be fun for either of us waiting for Maddy to come back out. Please, I'm not asking you for me—I'm asking you for them."

Rowan sucked in her bottom lip, tugging on Kyle's arm. He nodded at her, and she smiled.

"Come in, Andrew," he said, scratching his head with his other hand. "There's a spare bed in Mia's room, we can put her down in there. Is she going to be okay waking up somewhere strange?"

I followed them in to the living room, and Rowan went around me to look at Carly's face. "Oh, Andrew. She's adorable."

"Spitting image of her mother," I said. I sat on the couch, and prised her arms from around my neck. "Carly, honey. I need you to wake up and meet some people."

Those big blue eyes opened, and I heard Rowan behind me make an *awww* sound. "Daddy?" Carly said, looking around.

"This is Rowan. If it's okay with you, I'm going to let you have your first sleepover with her."

She frowned, her fingers digging into me. "Carly, I have to look after Mummy. Rowan has a bed you can sleep in that's much more comfortable than sleeping on me. And she has a little boy for you to play with in the morning that's the same age as you."

At that, her eyes widened. She played with other children at the group Maddy took her to sometimes, but the idea of a child to play with just her would be exciting.

"That's right, Carly. Charlie is the same age as you, and he has a big sister, Mia. They'll both be very excited to meet you. And we can all have pancakes for breakfast if you want." Rowan took a step forward, and smiled that magic smile at Carly.

Carly nodded, her grip relaxing as she smiled back.

"I'll be back in the morning to pick you up and take you to see Mummy. Okay?" I tapped her on the nose, and she grinned.

"I might even have some hot chocolate in the kitchen to help you sleep." Rowan kept that smile up. When she did that, she could talk anyone into just about anything.

Carly raised her hand to her mouth, sucking on a finger and I knew she was gathering the courage to ask something. She was bold like her mother, but had her bashful moments.

"What is it, Carly?" Rowan asked. Of course, if anyone knew that shy look, it was her.

"Is Mia awake?"

Rowan shook her head. "It's late, sweetie. Mia's fast asleep, but she'll be up in the morning and you can play together." She reached out, and ran her hand over Carly's curls. "Come on, I'll get you sorted."

She stood, and smiled at me. "I'll take care of her; don't worry about it. Just go and make sure Maddy is okay."

Kyle swayed on his heels, clearly not comfortable with me being here. "Thanks so much, both of you. I know I'm the last person you want to see, but I knew I could trust you to look after my baby girl."

At that, Kyle relaxed for some reason. I don't know, but his face softened at my words, and he nodded.

"I understand. We're lucky that we have my dad around. She'll be fine here. We'll take good care of her and take as long as you need," he said.

"Thank you." I nodded, turning towards the door.

Two steps later, I had blonde curls against my hand as my daughter threw herself at my leg. "Daddy," she cried.

I bent, and she wrapped her little arms around me. Closing my eyes, I took a deep breath of her hair, smelling that baby scent.

"You be a good girl for Rowan, and I'll come and get you in the morning," I whispered, pushing the strands of hair off her face that had escaped her ponytail. She cupped my face in her hands, pursing her lips for a kiss.

"Love you, Carly." I kissed her, and she snuggled against my neck.

"Love you too, Daddy," she said before letting go.

Rowan extended her hand to Carly, and she ran to her. "My mummy is sick," she announced loudly.

"I know, sweetie. So we're going to find lots of things to keep you busy while she gets better," Rowan said. She met my eye, looking more like the old Rowan, but with much more confidence than she ever had before. I guessed that came from being with the right person.

Thank you. I mouthed the words, and she led Carly into the kitchen.

"Good luck," Kyle said. "How about we swap numbers so you can get hold of us and vice versa."

In my haste to get back to Maddy, I hadn't even thought about that. "Sure."

It felt weird swapping phone numbers with the person who must hate me more than anyone else in the world, but at the same time I was glad he could put that aside to help Carly. I was eternally grateful for that.

As I pulled in to the hospital car park, my phone buzzed.

I've given her hot chocolate. She's already asleep. Rowan.

I clutched my phone to my chest. Now to make sure Maddy was okay.

THIRTY-FIVE

"WHERE'S MY BABY?" she asked, glaring at me as I walked in the door. A nurse was inserting a cannula in the back of her hand so they could monitor her. She winced as the needle went in.

"She's safe." I raised my eyes to the ceiling so I didn't have to meet her eyes. "She's with Rowan."

"She's what?" Maddy screeched. I looked back down as the nurse jumped from the sudden noise. "Andrew, you could have gotten in big trouble for going near her."

"I knew that, but you two are far more important to me. Besides, she and Kyle were glad to help. Carly's snuggled in a warm bed, having had hot chocolate, and has other kids to play with in the morning to keep her mind off you."

I reached for Maddy's face, stroking her cheek with my fingers as she closed her eyes.

"Is she really safe there? I mean, they don't really have any reason to help you and every reason to get back at you." She kissed my hand, opening her eyes and looking up at me. Her eyes searched my face for an answer.

I nodded. "I would never have gone near them if I didn't think I needed to, but Rowan will take good care of her. She was always the one who tried to rescue half-dead birds in the orchard and tried to nurse them back to health."

"Carly wasn't upset at you leaving her there?"

I shrugged. "She was half-asleep so that probably made it easier. You should have seen her at the thought that there were other children there. That woke her up. She was so tired, Rowan said she went straight to sleep."

I handed her my phone so she could see the text from Rowan the night before.

Her face softened as she read it, some of the worry fading away. "I love that she sent you this. Just to know that Carly was asleep and not upset."

"You know Carly; she would have slept on the lino in here if she'd had to."

Maddy laughed. We were always picking Carly up from the floor where she'd fallen asleep. Any place, many awkward positions.

"I suppose I should be happy that she slept in a bed."

I leaned forward, kissing her on the nose. "Well, there you go. Now, let's get you sorted so we can all be together."

Moments later, two nurses came to get Maddy for surgery. I'd made it back just in time, but now came the wait.

I squeezed her hand, and she squeezed back. We shared more love gazing at each other for those scant seconds than some people get in a lifetime.

It was that look I'd envied between Mum and Dad.

We had it.

SITTING ALONE IN THE ROOM, all I could think about was Maddy. Everything that came before her hadn't lost any importance, but now, she was the whole world to me.

She'd pushed her way into my life with all the heat of the sun.

My world had fallen apart, but she put it back together again, piece by piece, until it all fell back into place and I found a reason to move forward.

The birth of Carly had brought us closer, even though we'd had to deal with the death of Maddy's mum. Our daughter had brought the joy back to her eyes, and given her a new passion. The thought of anything happening to Maddy gave me a stomach-ache.

She was my wife, my lover—my best friend. Everything I was revolved around her. Now, I waited for the news that she had come out okay. I didn't care if we could never have another child, although I knew that would be so hard on Maddy. I had all I needed, and I'd spend the rest of my life showing her.

The constant ticking of the wall clock started to grate on my nerves as the time passed. I closed my eyes, burying my face in my hands to avoid looking at how long she'd been in surgery.

I just wanted to take her home and hold her, love her, every single day for the rest of my life. Maybe we could move closer to Mum and Dad, give Carly easier access to her grandparents. Getting a house would be cheaper there than it had been in the big city, and Maddy could relax and get back into her music.

Doing that would be hard, though; we loved our little house. It had become a home with Carly, and it was the only home she had ever known. So many things to think about.

I HAD no idea how much time had gone by, losing myself in thought about how we could move forward as a family. Maddy had been so cranky and we'd fought so much the last few weeks. Now I understood just how much her health had been affecting her, even if she hadn't realised.

Finally the doors opened, and they wheeled her back into the room. I stood back while they made her comfortable, waiting patiently, even though I just wanted to hold her and tell her just how much I loved her.

She was still drowsy, and a nurse smiled at me as she left. "I don't think you're supposed to be in here, but I won't say anything. She'll be sleepy for a while longer, but everything went well and the doctor will be 'round in the morning to talk to both of you."

"Thank you," I said, never taking my eyes off Maddy.

She stirred, her eyes opening at the sound of my voice, a faint smile appearing on her lips. "You're here."

"Where else would I be?" I said. I moved to sit on the bed at her side, kissing her on the forehead.

"I'm so sleepy."

"Then sleep. I'll be right beside the bed."

"Love you," she mumbled.

"Love you too." She was already gone, sleeping soundly, and I sat back in the chair beside the bed. Whatever had happened, we'd get all the details in the morning together. There would be no baby this time, but what the future held would become clearer when the doctor told us how bad it was.

Maddy was safe, and that was all that mattered to me. How she'd take the loss of the baby was another matter.

I RUBBED the stubble on my chin as my five o'clock shadow started to creep out. Distracted by our argument last night, I hadn't shaved before bed as I usually did. Maddy often joked about it making me look more rugged when I forgot, but I liked staying tidy for her. Besides, when she ran her lips under my chin and down my bare neck, it did things to me that I couldn't even begin to explain.

Her eyes opened slowly, they were bleary, but it was so good to look into the darkness that I loved so much.

"Hey," she murmured.

"Morning." I took her hand in mine, raising it to my lips.

"You need a shave."

I shook my head, laughing. "You never skip a beat do you?"

"If I don't tell you what to do, who else is going to?" She rolled onto her side towards me, her tired eyes full of love.

"I'd just fall apart without you, Maddy. You know it." I planted more kisses on her hand.

"Did they tell you what happened in surgery?" she asked.

I shook my head. "Not yet. The nurse said it went well, but that the doctor would be around this morning to talk to us. I think they just wanted you to get some sleep."

"I feel empty," she whispered, tears pricking her eyes.

"I know. We'll see what the doctor says and go from there. And once we've spoken to the doctor, I'll go and get Carly. Pretty sure having her around will make you feel better."

Maddy nodded, squeezing my hand. "Do you think she's okay? Being somewhere strange?"

"She has kids to play with, and they're having pancakes this morning."

Maddy smiled wanly. "She'll like that. I hate that we had nowhere else for her to go."

I sighed, stroking her face with my fingers. "I know. But I'd rather she was there than here, and going through all this with us. She's got other children to play with and things to distract her. I'm sure she'll be excited to see me and come and see you, but she'll be okay for the moment."

"THE GOOD NEWS is that we didn't have to do anything with the fallopian tube," the doctor said. Maddy had been gripping my hand tightly since he'd walked in the door, and that lessened as she received the news she'd been hoping for.

She closed her eyes.

"So, what now?" I asked.

"We need to monitor Maddy's hormone levels, make sure they're back to normal. If you're planning on trying again, it's best to wait until this pregnancy is completely out of her system. I'd suggest at least three months."

"Thank you," she whispered.

"The nurse will bring around some more information on counselling and support if you need it. I would suggest resting up for a while, letting someone else take care of things."

I squeezed her hand. "I'll take some time off, look after you and Carly for a while."

Maddy pulled her hand away, raising it to my face and smiling that pale smile that told me everything would be alright, but not just yet. She needed time.

"Anything else you need, just let the nurse know. We'll move you to a ward shortly; we just need to keep an eye on you for a couple of days."

"Thanks, Doctor," I said. I'd rather Maddy was in my arms tonight, safe and sound, right where I needed her to be. Even one night without her was one night too much.

"Can you go and get Carly?" she asked.

"Of course I can."

THIRTY-SIX

THE SOUND of children giggling floated through the air as I approached the front door. Kyle opened the front door to my knock, covered in flour and shaking his head in amusement as I stifled a laugh.

"Go ahead. You can laugh too. Your daughter certainly thought it was funny enough for the three of them to gang up on me and do this."

"I'm so sorry, Kyle," I said between laughs.

He shrugged. "Life with kids. Carly's fitting in well, but she'll be pleased to see you."

A screech came from behind him, and Carly came flying out the door and into my arms. "Daddy," she squealed.

"Hey." I swung her around, and she giggled in delight.

"We was making pancakes." She hugged me tight, and I kissed her cheek before wiping flour from her nose.

"Well, some of us were making pancakes. The rest were throwing flour," Kyle said. "Come in, Andrew. Have you had breakfast?"

I shook my head. "I've been beside Maddy's bed all night. They brought breakfast in for her, but I made her eat the whole lot."

Carly wriggled in my arms, and I dropped her on the ground so she could run back inside. Following Kyle, I saw what a mess they'd made.

They were all covered in various amounts of flour. It was all over the kitchen floor, the cupboards, and the counter. Rowan, who would have shrieked at the thought of being so messy when we were younger, was sitting on the floor, laughing as her youngest threw a tiny handful of flour at her.

"Enough you guys," Kyle said. "Let me finish up in here and we'll have some breakfast. You're welcome to join us, Andrew. If this lot don't eat them all, you could even take some for Maddy."

"Aww, Daddy." Rowan joined in the chorus from the kids, and Kyle cocked an eyebrow at her. The way she looked at him told the whole story about how in love they were. That and the fact that he was about to clean up the mess she'd helped make.

He held out his hand, and she took it as he pulled her up off the floor.

"Okay, okay," she said. "I'll take the kids to go and wash up."

There was a blur of movement as their two children with mine in tow ran past, Rowan following behind. I shook my head, grinning at the sight of them.

"I dropped some flour on the floor and next thing it was everywhere." Kyle laughed.

"If you've got a vacuum cleaner, I'm happy to help clean it up. I'm sure my girl was in on it too."

He opened a cupboard and pulled one out. "I am not going to say no to some free labour."

I took it from him, grinning as he pointed out where to plug it in. "I never thought I'd be vacuuming your floor, of all things."

"I never thought you'd be in my house again." His eyes locked on mine, a warning contained within.

"It wasn't something I planned either. I really do appreciate everything you've done. Maddy does too. Well, she did after recovering from the shock that I'd come here. I was scared as hell last night, and knowing Carly would be looked after really helped."

He nodded, the look in his eyes softening. "How's Maddy?"

"Desperate to get out of hospital. But okay. They didn't have to remove a fallopian tube, which was what she was scared of. She's been through so much in her life, it just sucks that she's had to deal with this too."

"I'm sorry to hear that, but glad she's on the mend."

I started the vacuum, sucking up all the flour as Kyle went back to making pancakes. We used to have pancakes on Saturday mornings at Rowan's place; her mother had what she called her secret recipe. They always tasted better than any other pancakes, though as I grew, I realised it wasn't the recipe that was so different—it was the fact it was a secret.

"Do you guys do this often?" I yelled over the sound of the vacuum.

"Rowan likes to do this every weekend, and we've kind of fallen into a routine with it. Usually it's not quite so messy. Carly enjoyed joining in with our kids, though. The three of them had a lot of fun throwing flour at me."

I laughed, shaking my head as the flour slowly started disappearing.

"What you doing, Daddy?" Carly's voice came from behind me, and I turned to see my daughter wrinkling up her nose at the sight of me cleaning, as if she hadn't seen it a million times before.

"Cleaning up after you," I said, waving the end of the vacuum at her. She squealed, running around in a circle before doubling over, laughing. At least she wasn't worried about Maddy, and seemed to have made herself completely at home.

"Carly's been such a good girl." Rowan came up behind her, running her hand down Carly's curls. Her eldest child stood behind her, dark hair and the same blue eyes her father had. *Mia.* I was about to say how great that was, but the words caught in my throat looking at Rowan's eldest. I'd taken her mother away from her when she was a baby, without a second thought for her needs.

Mia blushed, hiding behind her mother, while Charlie, Rowan's youngest, grabbed Carly's hand. "Come and play."

Carly shook her head. "My daddy here." She pointed at me, and I screwed up my face, prompting her to copy. We were in our own little world, despite the other family surrounding us. I loved this kid so damn much.

"My daddy here too," Charlie said, pointing at Kyle.

"The pancakes will be really soon, guys. Why don't you all go and sit at the table?" Kyle said.

Rowan held out her hand for Carly to take, and Carly looked towards me, as if to ask what she should do.

"Go on. I'll be there in a minute."

She nodded, taking Rowan's hand. Rowan led her and the other children to the table to sit and wait, and I grinned at her organisational skills. It was so her.

I looked up to see Kyle studying me, his face emotionless, just observing how I reacted to his wife.

"I bet she keeps you lot in line," I said.

His face cracked as he broke into a smile. "You know she does."

"Maddy's the same. What she says goes. Carly and I know better than to argue."

The grin spread across his face as he nodded. "I bet."

He turned back to the frying pan. "I'm looking forward to meeting this woman who tamed you. If she's anything like Carly ..." He looked over his shoulder. "She'll be a real charmer."

"Maddy is very charming." I grinned, meeting his eyes where I found unexpected warmth. Maybe I could win him over.

I moved to the table where the children were waiting. Rowan sat at the head of the table with Carly on one side and Charlie on the other. The two youngest ones were poking tongues at one another while Mia rolled her eyes and tucked a paper napkin into the neck of her shirt.

When I sat next to Carly, she laughed loudly. "My daddy is going to eat pancakes too." I shook my head at her shrill giggle.

"Shhh, Carly."

The table had been set with plastic plates for the children, and Rowan got up, retrieving another from the kitchen for me.

"Thanks, I think," I said with a laugh.

"You got a kids plate, Daddy?" Carly asked.

"Yes, I do." I leaned over and kissed her on the nose, making her giggle some more.

She grinned, and I moved my chair closer to hers. She snuggled up to me, and I looked down at her with a smile.

Kyle appeared in the doorway with a huge pile of pancakes. He placed them in the centre of the table. "Dig in everybody."

I filled Carly's plate first, before grabbing a pancake for myself. Just the one and then we'd be out of here.

Carly ate with great enthusiasm, wolfing down the pancakes and emptying her plate before licking it clean. I laughed, shaking my head, getting a cheeky grin in return.

"Yummy," she declared, holding her plate out for me.

"Anyone would think you'd never been fed." I tapped her on the nose, grabbing another pancake off the serving platter in the centre of the table with my fork and placing it on the plate. Rowan picked up the bottle of maple syrup and dropped some on the pancake. The maple syrup dribbled over the edges and onto the plastic. More for her to lick.

"It's been a big morning. They were all up early." Rowan laughed. "Mia was thrilled to find Carly in her room. I think she thought she finally had a little sister."

"No such luck, Mia," I said, grinning at the little girl. She smiled bashfully. "I bet you like having a little brother, though."

Mia laughed behind her hand. "Not all the time."

She was so reminiscent of Rowan as a child—all the same mannerisms, the same way of speaking. Rowan had been my best friend at that age.

"Mia looks so much like you," I said, smiling at Rowan. "Same as this one and Maddy."

I looked at Carly. She'd managed to get syrup on her face and was trying to touch her tongue to her nose to lick it off.

"All the grace of your mother, too." I reached over, wiping Carly's nose with a tissue.

Carly giggled. "Daddy."

"We need to get going soon. Mummy wants to see you."

"She in the hostibal?"

I nodded. "Yes, but she's all better now. Not so cranky. But she's going to need a lot of cuddles and looking after."

Carly beamed. "I can do that."

Rowan and Kyle laughed. "I'm sure you will, sweetheart," Kyle said.

"Seriously, Andrew. While Maddy's recovering, Carly's welcome any time." Rowan said.

"Don't you have a job?" I grinned at her while she laughed.

"Working for family has its perks." Rowan and Kyle exchanged a loving look as she said the words. "I still work for Kyle's father."

"And she's the boss, so gets to work flexible hours. Most of the time she's working on her laptop remotely while the kids run riot," Kyle said.

I laughed. "That's great. I'm sure the kids love having her around. Maddy hasn't worked since we had Carly. It's tight, but we manage, so I'm happy for her to do what she wants, and Carly loves it."

"Mummy plays music," Carly yelled.

"Shhh, Carly. Maddy's a violinist. I've been trying to convince her to apply for a post in the regional orchestra. I think it'll do her some good. Especially now."

"That's so cool." Rowan smiled. My girls were definitely helping to thaw relations between all of us. It was weird, but wonderful.

When we were finished, Kyle stood and picked up the platter. "There's a couple left. Want me to put them on a plate with some plastic wrap and you can take them to Maddy?"

"Mummy likes pancakes," Carly said.

"She does. That would be great." Standing, I picked up my plate and then Carly's.

"Leave them there," said Rowan, "I'll sort them out. You did help clean up after this lot before."

I laughed. "Considering my daughter was responsible for part of that mess, it was the least I could do."

Kyle returned with two rolled pancakes on a plastic plate. "Here, I made the assumption she'd like maple syrup."

I took the plate from his hands. "Thank you so much. I'm sure she'll love them. That's if they survive the trip in the car with this one." I nodded towards Carly, who was pulling her lower lip almost down to her chin, laughing with Charlie.

"Hey, baby, we have to go and see Mummy. Do you want to say thank you to Rowan and Kyle and goodbye to the others?"

She nodded, her lips downturned as she looked at Rowan.

"Thank you," she said.

Rowan lit up, moving around the table to Carly's chair. "You are very welcome. If your Mummy wants to bring you around to play any time, we'd love to see you again."

Carly hugged her, Rowan looking over Carly's shoulder at me. "We mean it, Andrew. You've got Kyle's number."

"I appreciate it more than you know," I said.

She smiled, standing and stepping out of the way so Carly could say goodbye to the others. My little girl looked miserable, but I knew once she was back with Maddy she'd be happy again.

Maddy had been moved to the ward when we returned, smiling as we walked in the door. Her eyelids still looked heavy, but her eyes were more beautiful than I remembered. We'd been at each other's throats the last few weeks rather than just enjoying being together that I'd almost forgotten how easy it was to get lost in them.

"Hey," she whispered.

"Mummy!" Carly stretched, reaching for her.

"Sweetheart, Mummy's going to be a bit sore for a while. We'll sit on the bed, but no jumping on her. Okay?"

She nodded, her big blue eyes wide now at the surroundings. There were four beds in the ward, and women occupied the other three, two of them with babies. One of the babies started crying, and I glanced at Maddy who looked towards the sound with tears in her eyes.

"It's a bit shit putting you in here with them," I muttered. I sat Carly on the bed beside Maddy and pulled the big circular curtain around to give us some privacy.

Maddy shrugged. "I guess we all gotta go somewhere." Carly snuggled in to Maddy's side, and I watched as Maddy took a deep breath into Carly's hair.

"The sooner you're home the better, as far as I'm concerned."

Maddy leaned back on the pillow. "I don't know why. I've not exactly been easy to live with."

"No, you're a pain in the butt, but I'm used to that now. Carly and I need you home, where we can take care of you."

A big smile spread across her face. She looked exhausted, and I knew I'd have to get Carly home soon—not that I wanted to leave Maddy here at all. We didn't speak. Neither of us could talk about what had happened, not yet. She didn't have to tell me how devastated she was this whole thing had occurred, and I didn't have to tell her how I'd been terrified of losing her. Somehow we conveyed all that to each other in that moment, just looking at one another.

"Did you have fun with the other kids?" Maddy asked Carly.

Carly nodded enthusiastically. "We made pancakes."

"I've even got a couple for you," I said, placing the plate on the cabinet beside the bed.

"Thank you. You must be exhausted."

"You look tired too."

Maddy reached for my hand, and I squeezed hers as I grabbed it. "I think we all need some sleep."

"Except for Carly. I've created a monster." I laughed as Maddy shook her head.

"Well, she'll have to be your problem for a couple of days."

"I think I can live with that." I leaned over, kissing Maddy softly, scared of breaking my fragile-looking woman.

My beautiful family was safe. I could live through anything.

THIRTY-SEVEN

MADDY WAS DISCHARGED on Monday morning, and Carly and I were overjoyed to be bringing her home. We'd missed her so much in our little house.

Guiding Maddy to the couch, I frowned as she sat.

"Lie down. I'll get a blanket," I said.

"I'm not an invalid," she snarled.

"Close enough. I took time off work for this—the least you can do is let me take care of you." I poked my tongue out, and a smile spread across her face.

I left the room to get a blanket, and when I returned she was lying down, a cushion under her head. Carly stood beside the couch, Maddy's palm stroking her cheek.

"You okay?" I asked.

Carly nodded, staring solemnly at her mother.

"Mum's just got to rest now. She'll be fine. We just have to look after her."

She nodded. "You're our 'sponsibility, Mummy."

Maddy smirked, pulling Carly's chin towards her face until they touched noses. "Yes, boss." She looked up at me, her eyes shining, sucking her lips in as if trying not to laugh.

"That's right. She is our responsibility. We need to take really good care of her," I said, meeting Maddy's gaze. *Love this woman so damn much.*

Carly nodded solemnly

Maddy's eyes, usually so full of life and emotion, were dead. The brief light I saw sparking in them with Carly had faded away by the evening, and she watched me as I climbed into bed beside her, pulling the blanket up and making sure she was covered.

"Come here," I said, sliding my arm under her neck. She closed her eyes briefly, opening them again to look at me. The purple smudges under her eyes showed just how much she needed rest. "You look so tired."

"It's hard to sleep in the hospital, and the only night we've spent apart since we were married was when Carly was born. I hated sleeping alone."

I raised my hand to her face, stroking her cheek. "You're back where you belong now. I was so scared, Maddy."

"All I could think about was you," she whispered. "I was so worried what you would do if anything happened to me. I know you have Carly to take care of, but …"

I gripped her chin with my hand, pulling her face closer to mine. "You are everything to me, Maddy. You and Carly. I can't imagine a world without either of you. I love you so much."

Kissing her softly, I moved back a little to look at her eyes. They gave away nothing, and I pulled her closer.

"I just need some sleep. I won't have any problems now I'm home with you."

She snuggled up to me, and I listened to her breathing as it slowed, the sound as familiar to me as her voice. It brought me reassurance that she was safe in my arms. Nothing could harm her here.

My own sleep called to me as the moments passed, and I gave up the fight, letting my eyes close and joining my wife in her slumber.

We were woken in the morning by Carly bouncing on the bed to greet her mother. I sat up, rubbing my eyes and yawning, shaking my head at her energy.

"Carly, leave your mother alone. She needs to rest."

"I'm fine." Maddy's sleepy voice said. "You two are the best medicine."

Carly walked to the head of the bed, sliding down under the blanket between us. She wrapped her arms around Maddy's neck, and Maddy grinned, hugging her tight.

"Good morning. Want to snuggle with me?"

Carly nodded. "I missed you when you were in the hostibal."

"I missed you too. But, I'm home now, so we can spend heaps of time together."

I stroked Carly's soft hair while she snuggled into Maddy. My two beautiful girls. Loving them was the easiest thing in the world to do, and we were all soon drifting asleep, cuddled up together.

When I woke again, the two of them were still both snoozing, and I slid out of bed as quietly as I could, on a mission to make pancakes for my sleeping beauties.

I stood in the kitchen, mixing the flour and eggs together, whipping them into a batter to cook when two warm hands slid up my bare chest.

"Hmm." Maddy nibbled on my neck.

"What are you up to?" I turned my head to kiss her.

"Feeling up my husband. He of the magnificent chest."

Her fingers stroked my skin, feeling every groove, exploring every inch of me.

"Maddy, you really need to stop doing that unless you really want me to throw you over my shoulder and ..."

She pulled me around to face her. "Maybe you should. Carly's fast asleep."

"You need to recover. I'm not about to risk hurting you more."

Maddy pouted, the beautiful lips I loved to kiss turning down at my rejection. I grasped her chin, tilting her head up towards me.

"Tonight, when she's has gone to sleep, I'll take you to bed and kiss every inch of you. Would that make you happy? I know it would make me happy."

She sighed. "I turn into a puddle when you look at me that way."

I bent my head to kiss her, touching my lips against hers ever so gently. "I hope that's always the case. Love you."

Wrapping her arms around my waist, she snuggled in against my chest. "I love you too."

The sudden scream of the smoke alarm caused her to yelp in surprise before bursting out laughing. The butter melting in the frying pan had burned out and the smoke rising off the cooktop had the alarm wailing.

She let go of me, while I grabbed the plastic handle of the frying pan, picking it up and dumping it into the sink of warm water waiting for the dishes.

We looked at each other, laughing as the pan fizzled in the water. I went into the living room and pressed the button on the alarm to stop the noise just as Carly came wandering out of the bedroom, her hands over her ears.

"You're so noisy," she scolded.

"Yes, I am." I bent and scooped her up into one arm, while reaching for Maddy with the other. "So, I think once I've cleaned up the mess I've made, I'm going to take you two out for pancakes."

"Can we see Mia and Charlie?" Her eyes widened.

"Mia and Charlie?" Maddy looked at me.

"Rowan's kids." I looked back at Carly. "Not today, sweetheart. I think it'll just be the three of us, and we'll take care of Mummy while she gets better."

"Oh." Her face fell, the disappointment obvious.

Maddy reached up to stroke her cheek. "Tell you what. During the week we could bake some cupcakes and take them around to Mia and Charlie's mum and dad to say thank you for you staying there."

Carly nodded, her little face lighting up at the idea.

"Are you sure about that?" I asked.

"They didn't have to help us, but they did. And I appreciate it. Besides, don't you think I'm a little curious about meeting Rowan?"

I kissed the top of her head, and laughed. "Maybe that's what I'm afraid of."

THIRTY-EIGHT

FOR THE FIRST TIME EVER, I came home to an empty house. No sign of Maddy or Carly; no noise, just the silence. I hated it.

Pulling my phone out of my pocket, I sent a quick text.

> Me: Where are you? I just got home.

Seconds later came the response.

> Maddy: Picking up fish and chips for dinner. I'm running a bit late.

I sat on the couch, flicking on the television. The news was full of awful, miserable stories and I stared at the screen, wondering just what kind of a world Carly would grow up in. At least within our own home she was loved, protected. Wherever she went in her life, I hoped that would always be the case.

She came screaming through the door, all curls and laughter. "Daddy," she screeched, jumping onto the couch and into my arms.

"Hey, baby girl."

"Mummy got me chicken nuggets with the chips."

I tickled her under the chin. "Did she now? Aren't you a lucky girl?"

"I don't know about her, but I'm planning on being lucky." Maddy leaned over the back of the couch, kissing me and waggling her eyebrows.

"We all lucky!" Carly exclaimed. Maddy dissolved into fits of laughter, taking her precious food parcel to the kitchen to serve.

"What did you get up to today?" I asked Carly as she snuggled under my arm.

"We saw Mia and Charlie."

"Did you now?" Maddy had asked for Rowan's address, but I didn't know if Maddy would go through with meeting her. This shouldn't have been a surprise, but it was.

"Mummy made chocolate cupcakes."

I tapped her on the nose. "You're double lucky, then. Come here."

Snuggling up on my lap, Carly kissed my cheek and I switched to a cartoon. No big, bad news stories for my little girl.

Maddy reappeared with three plates. "Screw sitting at the table," she said, placing mine in front of me on the coffee table.

Carly took hers sitting on my lap, and we sat and watched some cartoon cat chase around a mouse as Maddy and Carly ate.

"Yours will get cold," Maddy said.

"I can wait. Carly's comfortable." I turned my head towards her, sharing the loving glance of a woman who surely must have me on a promise. She pursed her lips, blowing me a kiss and turned back to the television while eating the rest of her dinner.

When Carly was finished, I bent and picked up my plate, moving it beside me on the couch. I picked at the food, Maddy and Carly snuggled up to me. Life couldn't get any better than this.

As Carly's eyes grew heavy, Maddy plucked her off my lap to get her changed and in to bed. The sound of running water and giggles while Carly cleaned her teeth made me smile.

Maddy was back a few minutes later, standing behind the couch.

"Seriously, those things are like sleeping pills for that child. We were teeth brushed, in bed, and she was comatose within minutes."

I laughed. "All the better for us."

I grabbed her, pulling her over the back of the sofa and into my arms. She giggled, and I stroked her face, kissing her gently, finding her tongue with mine, my free hand stroking her body.

"She is amazing, Andrew. So beautiful, so free," Maddy said.

"Just like her mother."

Maddy pulled me down for another kiss, the palm of her hand resting on my cheek.

"Love you, Maddy," I whispered.

Her lips replied with gentle kisses that left me floating. No matter how long we spent together, the buzz was always new, unrelenting. Mere contact kept me feeling so alive.

"I KNOW WHY YOU LOVED HER," Maddy whispered. Our limbs were still tangled from our frantic love-making, her bare skin so soft against mine.

"What? Who?"

"Rowan. She's just so nice. Sweet and caring."

I laughed. "She could go to anywhere in the world and make friends."

"Do you still love her?"

Her eyes were sad, as if she didn't want to hear the response, but I couldn't lie.

"I'll always love her. Just like I'll always be in love with you. You would have seen how well the kids got on? That's what we were like. Joined at the hip."

"Rowan and I hit it off, but I think we're polar opposites." She ran her finger down my chest in the way that made me hold my breath while my blood stirred parts down below.

"You don't think you're sweet? I think you have a lot of similarities. You're infinitely more outgoing than she is, but you both have big hearts."

Flattening her palm, she looked up at me with a sly grin. "That husband of hers is pretty hot too."

"Oh, really?" I reached for her hand, moving further down where she could feel the results of her efforts.

Her chest heaved as her breathing sped up, her fingers exploring just how hard I was.

"Not as hot as my husband, though. You let me lick your abs, after all." Bending her head to kiss my chest, her hand tightened around me, and I threw my head back onto the pillow as she worked her magic.

"You can lick me anywhere." I gasped, reaching for her, pulling her on top of me.

"In a hurry?"

"I am when you touch me like that."

Sitting astride me, she slid down onto me, and that warm, familiar feeling of her engulfed me. She was the only woman I ever wanted to be intimate with now. Everything I had and everything I was belonged to her.

She looked so beautiful, carefree, that summer smile of hers lighting up my soul, setting me afire with the love that burned between us. Our everlasting flame.

THIRTY-NINE

I KNEW the phone was ringing, but had no idea where it was. It must have been buried in paperwork; the sound grew louder the further down I dug towards the desk.

Eager to get it before it went to voicemail, I didn't even look at the caller ID. Chances were that it was Maddy, anyway. Sometimes she called me just to heavy breathe down the phone.

"Andrew Carmichael."

"Andrew, it's Rowan."

I tried to speak, tripping over my tongue to say anything else. *Get it together.*

"Oh, hey. How are you?"

"I'm good. I was just calling to get Maddy's number off you. After she left, I realised I should have grabbed her number to keep in touch. We were going to the zoo this afternoon, and I know it's late notice, but I wondered if she and Carly wanted to come."

I was blown away, swallowing down the laugh that threatened to burst out. Now she wanted to be friends with Maddy. It was wonderful. The idea of having Rowan back in my life as a friend was better than anything I could have ever hoped for. But I didn't know if I wanted Maddy to spill all the beans about our relationship.

I guess having that beats not having her in my life at all.

"Sure. I'll text you her number. I'm not sure if she had plans today, she kind of does what she wants."

Rowan laughed. "She doesn't seem the type to let *you* boss her around."

"I couldn't win if I tried. But I wouldn't have it any other way."

This was how it used to be, the ease between us. Back before I screwed it all up.

"I don't know. If she's anything like me, she'll let you win, even if you don't realise you have."

I rolled my eyes. "That'd be right."

"Anyway, gotta go. Thanks, Andrew."

I hung up, texting her the number before placing the phone down. Maddy didn't have a lot of close friends. *I wonder if you two will become as close as Charlie and Rowan once were.*

It did me no good, thinking of the past. If the two of them became friends, it would be good for Maddy. That was what mattered.

Rowan's car was in the driveway when I pulled up to the house, with Maddy's alongside it. I parked on the road outside so Rowan could get out, marvelling at the thought of her being in my home. The world had turned upside down.

Laughter hit me as soon as I opened the door. Maddy sat with Rowan on the couch, coffee cups long emptied, giggling at something.

"Babe! We were just talking about you," Maddy said. I cocked an eyebrow, looking back and forward between the two women, unsure of what to say next.

"Am I safe?" I asked.

They burst out laughing, and Rowan nodded. "Perfectly safe. I should get my children out of here and home, though. Kyle will be wondering where I've gotten to."

As if on cue, a beep came from her bag, and she fished her phone out, nodding at it. "Yep, that's him."

She lost herself in the phone, replying to the message. Maddy beckoned me closer, and I bent to kiss her. She grabbed hold of my tie, pulling me down into a kiss that I can only describe as not appropriate for public viewing.

When she let me go, I turned my head to see Rowan smirking. "Oh, you two are so cute. I need to get home. Kyle's started dinner, but I don't want to be too late."

She stood, calling towards the bedrooms. "Mia, Charlie. Come on. We have to get home to Daddy."

"I'm kinda surprised to see you here," I said.

She shrugged. "We all had a great afternoon. Next time, you and Kyle should come with us."

Her suggestion made me grin. Kyle had been polite and understanding, but I didn't think he'd put up with my presence for too long.

"Come over for a barbecue at the weekend. The weather is supposed to be nice, and the kids can all play together until they fall asleep," Rowan said.

"That sounds great." Maddy beamed at me.

"Sure. Why not?" I flopped on a chair, sitting opposite the pair of them.

Out of nowhere, a mop of blonde curls were in my face as Carly threw herself up onto my lap. "We saw the tigers today, Daddy." She roared, clawing at me as I laughed.

"I think you might have brought a tiger home with you, Maddy," I said as Carly nuzzled my nose with her own.

"Carly is adorable." Rowan was smiling at me, and for the first time I saw the warmth I used to see. Back when we were friends.

"I kind of like her." The little hands were clawing at my chest. "Though not when I'm being clawed to pieces by a tiger," I said.

I growled at her, and she giggled as I stood, swinging her up before settling her on my hip. She snuggled into my neck.

"Daddy." She laughed.

"Rowan, Mia and Charlie are going home now. Do you want to say goodbye?" She nodded, pouting as I let her drop to the ground.

Rowan knelt down in front of her. "We'll see you another day. Very soon."

Carly nodded, jumping up and down and clapping her hands.

"See you at the weekend, then?" Rowan said to me.

"Yes, we'll see you at the weekend. We'd love to be there."

"Good."

She stood, smiling at both of us. "We'll look forward to it."

Maddy came back inside after showing her to her car, and threw my car keys at me. "I moved your car into the driveway."

"You didn't have to."

She looked around. "Where's Carly?"

"Gone back to her room. She said she was tired."

Maddy straddled my lap, leaning in for a kiss. "She might be tired, but I'm not," she whispered.

I ran my hands down her back, palms first, trailing my thumbs behind. "Neither am I." I waggled my eyebrows at her while she laughed, her arms draped over my shoulders, snuggling up to me.

"Mummy," Carly called.

Maddy sighed, pinching my neck between her fingers.

"That feels good, do it some more?"

"Later." She kissed me before backing off me and heading off to Carly's room.

I watched as she walked away. I was crazy about her, and it was so good to see her so happy again.

Barbecue at Rowan's at the weekend. My life could not get any more bizarre.

FORTY

IT WASN'T ENOUGH.

Despite her growing friendship with Rowan, Maddy still seemed so empty at times, and I knew she mourned the loss of our baby, just as I did.

Rowan had lost a baby too, she'd told Maddy that the first day they'd met. It gave Maddy comfort to have a friend who had been through something similar.

We were due at their place at the weekend, and I was nervous beyond belief.

Mid-week, I was struck by inspiration, and came home from work early to complete the project I'd just created. Maddy stood by, cocking an eyebrow at me as I dismantled the bed in the spare room, moving it to the garage.

"What are you doing?" she asked.

"Something for you. Just wait."

Right down the back of the garage, there were unopened boxes from our move, and as soon as she saw them coming in the door, she smiled slightly.

"What are they, Mummy?" Carly asked.

She shook her head. "A thing of the past."

"A thing of the future," I said, ripping open the first box.

Her violin case came first, followed by a music stand. Then her guitar and accompanying stand, and I set them up in the room. Carly's eyes were wide as dinner plates as she watched.

"It's a 'tar," she said.

"Yes, sweetie. Ask Mummy to play you a song." I smiled at her as she tugged at her mother's skirt.

"What is all this in aid of?" Maddy asked.

I stood, pulling the boxes apart, destroying them so she couldn't pack it all up again.

"I checked online. Orchestra auditions are coming up."

She rolled her eyes. "And?"

"And, Mrs Carmichael, it's time you lived your dream. So, I set you up a practice room."

She crossed the room, pulling the cardboard from my hands, her lips pressing against mine.

"I love you," she whispered.

"I love you too. I remember the look on your face when my mother said that Dad had given up music. I don't want you to ever think you have to. It's a part of you, Maddy. Just as much as Carly and I are."

Maddy flung her arms around my neck, holding on tight. I closed my eyes as she pressed her body against mine.

"Mummy, Mummy, play me a song."

"Anything you want." She smiled down at Carly, and let go of me, picking up her guitar and going out to the living room.

Carly trailed behind, and I soon heard the melodic sounds of Maddy's guitar as she played for our daughter.

I stood at the door, watching them. Carly was entranced, clapping and dancing as Maddy played song after song.

I didn't have to ask Maddy if this was therapeutic. The answer was written all over her face at the joy of sharing her talent with her daughter.

I also didn't have to ask how happy it made her. After dinner, she tucked Carly into bed, and from the spare room the soulful sound of the violin could be heard. I had no idea what she was playing. It was vaguely familiar, from some long-forgotten school music lesson.

Lying down on the couch, I rested my head on the arm, closing my eyes as the haunting music lulled me to sleep. It was beautiful, and so was she.

I woke to her straddling my hips awkwardly, the couch not being wide enough to hold both of us in that position.

"What are you doing?" I asked.

She leaned over, kissing me long and lingering. "Thanking you for what you did. Maybe I tried to suppress how much I missed it, but knowing you support me makes me very happy."

I reached up, running my hands down her arms. "I want you to be happy, Maddy. And I know this is what does it. Besides, I thought it would be good for you after everything."

Maddy kissed me again, running her fingers through my hair.

"You did good, Carmichael," she whispered.

"I'm glad. I loved hearing you play, and Carly's a big fan."

She laughed, sitting back up. "She had so much fun. When she's bigger, I'll teach her to play."

"Play for me," I whispered.

Our eyes locked and she kissed me, lingering again but so tender.

Climbing off my lap, she disappeared, and returned to stand in front of me with her violin. The music was so sweet and gentle, and I grinned as she closed her eyes, becoming lost in the sound.

This was her dream, and I'd move heaven and earth to make it come true for her.

FORTY-ONE

COMING BACK to Rowan's house again was weird. Part of me wanted to turn the car around and go, terrified of the memories.

But, she had taken such good care of my daughter and I would be eternally grateful.

Rowan answered the door, waving us into the living room. Carly screeched as she laid eyes on Charlie and ran past me and out to the deck where Kyle stood over the barbecue.

"Oh well, kids have found each other." Maddy laughed, shaking her head.

"Come out into the sunshine," Rowan said. "It's such a gorgeous day."

We followed her out, and I nodded at Kyle. He returned the gesture and went back to scrubbing the hot plate.

"You know, it would have been much smarter of me to clean this the last time we used it," he said, turning towards Rowan.

"I hate to say I told you so." Rowan sat back down, grinning.

He rolled his eyes, and kept scrubbing.

"Do you two want a drink? I just made coffee, or we have juice in the fridge."

"A juice would be great," said Maddy.

Rowan looked at me. "What about you?"

Our eyes met, and my mouth went dry, forming words an issue all of a sudden. This was too much.

Maddy leaned towards me. "Are you okay?"

I licked my lips, looking for moisture. "Yeah, sure. Juice is fine, Rowan."

She smiled, standing and leaving us there with Kyle.

Carly ran past. They were playing tag and Mia had the advantage, being bigger. She seemed to be letting the younger children win, surrendering to both of them. The cries of "tag, you're it" echoed through the backyard.

Maddy reached for my hand, squeezing it. "Are you really okay?"

I shrugged. "It's just all a bit weird. I'll be fine."

"I guess it will be for a while. Relax, babe. We wouldn't be here if they weren't okay with it," she whispered.

Rowan returned, glasses in hand. She set them down on the table and smiled at us. "I hope this isn't too weird," she said. She was always good at reading my mind.

Maddy shook her head. "We're good. Look at those three; they're best of buddies." The kids all ran past us again, Carly in pursuit of the other two. Mia came to a stop, pretending to hurt her ankle so Carly could tag her. She was a good kid.

"Mia's so good with the younger ones," Maddy said.

"She's very grown up for her age. Always has been." Rowan raised her face to the approaching Kyle, who had finished his cleaning task. He leaned in for a kiss, and she waggled her eyebrows at him.

"Ah, so what's what got you cleaning." The teasing words were out of my mouth before I could stop them.

All three of them burst out laughing, and I shrugged. "Works for me." I gazed at Maddy.

"Works for me too," said Kyle. He cocked his head at Rowan. "Is the food ready? The barbecue is ready to go."

"It's all in the fridge." She moved to stand and he gently pushed her back down.

"No, I'll get it. You stay here and entertain the guests."

I watched him go inside. Part of me wanted to reach out and try to be friends for the sake of our wives, but another part was afraid it would all turn sour.

Instead I stood, stepping off the deck and onto the grass. It was lovely, play equipment for the children, a sandpit, and I shook my head at the tree by the swings.

Venturing out, I leapt back as Mia nearly slammed into me. She looked up at me with those big blue eyes of her father's. "Sorry," she said.

"No worries, sweetheart."

Stopping helped Carly catch up and she threw herself at Mia to tag her. The pair of them went down in a heap with a fit of laughter.

"Carly, don't play so rough," I said, holding out my hand for her.

She took it, pulling herself to her feet and brushing her hair out of her eyes. Mia sat on the ground and I offered her the other hand, helping her up.

"Why don't you go and find something a bit more peaceful to do? Maybe Mia and Charlie have some toys."

"We've got some trucks and cars to play with," Mia said.

"Well, there you go. I'm sure dinner won't take long to cook and you guys can all be ready to eat. Are you hungry?"

The two heads nodded in unison.

"Charlie," Mia called.

Her brother appeared from his hiding place behind the garden shed.

"We're going to play with the cars," Mia said matter-of-factly. So like her mother.

He seemed to like the idea, sprinting past us and into the house. I shook my head as the other two ran after him. At least Carly would sleep well tonight.

"Did you see my tree?" Rowan's voice drifted toward me as she approached.

I made my way to my target, circling the tree, and raising an eyebrow at Rowan.

"How on earth did you find an apple tree in the middle of the city?" I laughed, pointing at the heart carved in the trunk with her and Kyle's initials.

She smiled. "I knew this was the right place when I found it." Running her fingers over the heart, she pulled her fingers against her palm as if trapping the feeling.

"You know there's a tree on your father's orchard with our initials carved into it," I said.

Raising her eyebrows, she looked straight into my eyes. "Really?"

"Yep. And one with mine and Charlie's initials, and probably one with your and Charlie's initials."

She laughed, slapping me on the arm. "You're probably right; we were all so close. I miss her so much, Andrew. That laugh of hers ... I don't think she ever thought a bad thing about anyone."

"There was never any bad in her, either. I miss her too. I let her down so badly. When she was alive, and in death. I'll never be able to make up for any of it."

Rowan's eyes misted up with tears, and she sucked in her lip. I knew that look.

"What is it?"

"You're here. I think that says a lot about what you've done to make up for it. Charlie would have wanted you to work it all out, be happy. I would say you've achieved that. You have a beautiful, loving family. That says so much about you."

"Shit." I looked at the ground, emotion welling up inside. I'd done it, shown them I wasn't who I used to be.

"What?" The concern in her voice was obvious.

"Damn women, always making me want to cry."

Rowan laughed, and I grinned up at her. "You have an amazing family too. Aren't we so grown up?" I said, locking eyes with her.

Maybe neither of us would ever forget what had happened, but more than ever it seemed like we could move past it.

Heavy footsteps came up behind me, and I turned to see Kyle, a beer in each hand.

"Want a beer?"

I nodded, smiling as I took it from his hand. "That sounds good to me."

"I did offer it to your wife first, but she tells me she's driving tonight."

Looking across at Maddy, I grinned as she raised her glass of orange juice at me. "Apparently so."

Kyle held up his beer. "Cheers, Andrew. Here's to our gorgeous families and whatever this is."

Rowan snuggled up to him as we clinked bottles together.

"There's something else we need to tell you," she said. She looked up at Kyle adoringly.

"Let me guess. You two are having another baby?"

Rowan shook her head. "We had the protection order cancelled. I figured that if Maddy and I are going to be friends, it would be nice if her husband could spend time with us legally."

I'd pushed all of that to the back of my mind the night I'd turned up here with Carly and never given it any more consideration, given Rowan and Kyle's hospitality after Kyle backed off.

"Thank you." I felt overwhelmed at the kindness of these two. "I don't know what else to say."

Kyle's hand landed on my shoulder. "It's very clear to us just how much you've changed. We know what Charlie's death did to you, Andrew. I have to be honest and tell you I didn't care if I never saw you again after I got Rowan back. But it's clear when you're with Maddy and Carly that you've moved on. We both see that."

I nodded, looking over at Maddy. She looked back quizzically, as if unsure if she should come over and see what we were talking about. The kids had hauled a box of cars out to the deck and were playing with them almost under her feet.

Our eyes locked, and I almost forgot the others were there. It was so easy to do that with Maddy. I worshipped the ground she walked on, and always would. She was my saviour as I was hers. We were just meant to be.

At the sight of what was on the barbecue, I laughed so hard Maddy thought there was something wrong with me.

"What on earth is so funny?" she asked as I doubled over.

"The kids are having barbecued chicken nuggets," I said. No one else would get our inside joke.

Maddy laughed.

"Rowan said Carly asked for them last time. She said they were her favourite food," Kyle said, exchanging a confused glance with Rowan.

"Carly will turn into a chicken nugget one day," I said.

"I not a chicken nugget, Daddy." Carly squawked.

"No, baby. You most certainly are not." I bent to pick her up, swinging her on my hip as she giggled.

"We can give them something else if you want," Rowan said.

I locked eyes with Maddy, the secret behind the smile safe.

"Chicken nuggets will be fine," I said.

Better than fine, she mouthed.

We were lost in each other for a moment, and I sat beside Maddy, pulling my chair closer to her.

I surveyed the scene—Kyle cooking on the barbecue with Rowan beside him, our children playing together, my amazing wife beside me.

All the pieces of my life coming together.

FORTY-TWO

SHE SIGHED as I lapped at her breasts, sucking gently on her nipples while my hand explored between her legs. "Andrew," she cried as her body tensed, begging for the release on its way.

I ignored her, my fingers playing her body like a musical instrument. *I'm the virtuoso of her body. I know just how she'll react to each stroke of my fingers, each flick of my tongue. I know her better than I've ever known anyone, and I'll never stop trying to learn more.*

"Andrew," she cried again, this time with more urgency, and again I ignored her, pushing my fingers into her where she needed it the most. She wanted more, but she'd have to wait just a little bit longer.

Her back arched as she cried out for me one more time before she convulsed in fits of pleasure, giving me what I wanted. My heart and soul belonged to her. Right at that moment, her body belonged to me.

"Maddy," I whispered, looking up at her face which said everything she felt without words. I rolled onto my back, stroking her arm. She needed no further invitation, straddling my hips, lowering herself onto me as I filled her.

"I love you," she whispered, leaning over to kiss me. I stroked her thighs before laughing and flipping her onto her back, still inside her.

"You're mine." I ran my hands up her body, pinning her arms to the bed as I began traversing her with my lips, still thrusting into her as hard as I could.

We collapsed in a sweaty mess, and I laughed as I lay beside her, pulling her into my embrace.

"See? Letting Carly eat chicken nuggets for dinner? Best decision I ever made," I said, with a grin.

She rolled her eyes. "I'd better let her eat them every night if that's what I get."

I laughed. "As long as I made you happy, Mrs Carmichael. That's all that matters."

She rubbed my arm, opening her mouth as if she wanted to say something before closing it again.

"What is it?" I asked.

"Spending time with Rowan today. What was it like? Is it weird?"

I squeezed her tight. "Not as weird as I thought it would be. It's almost like we were before all this happened, back even before she found out about Charlie and I. Both Kyle and Rowan have shown a lot of faith in me, and I don't plan on letting them down. After everything that happened, too."

"That must feel like an eternity ago," Maddy whispered, snuggling in to me.

"It does. I was in such a deep, dark place when it all happened, and I can't pretend it didn't bother me for a long time that I couldn't reach out to my best friend anymore. But I found a new best friend, and I wouldn't change her for anything now."

"Oh," Maddy said, nodding.

"What?"

"Who is she?" She looked at me with that damn innocent look of hers, making me laugh out loud.

"Some woman who was crazy enough to hook up with an ex-crim. I don't know, maybe she needs her head read."

She nuzzled my chest. "I don't know, I think I did okay."

"Love you, Maddy Carmichael," I said.

She looked up at me, her eyes shining with love. "I might be a bit screwed up at times, but I love you too. Enough to keep you around for a little while longer anyway."

"Glad I'm useful for something, then," I said.

"You're useful for a lot of things. Speaking of which, I think it's time to try one of those things again."

I gaped at her. "Are you suggesting more sex?"

"If it's as good as that last lot, yes. Get moving, I'll rate you."

I laughed, kissing her, not wanting to ever let her go. "You are the best thing that could have ever happened to me," I whispered, hugging her tight.

"Let's just have sex for fun for a while, forget about any baby-making," she said.

Her hand moved down to my thigh, stirring me into action again.

"You know, I think that's just about the best idea you've ever had."

"You ain't seen nothing yet," she said with a grin.

FORTY-THREE

I HANDED her the envelope I'd retrieved from the letterbox. It looked official. This was it, whether or not the orchestra had accepted her application for an audition.

She took a deep breath, and turned it over to open it.

"No, I can't," she said, shaking her head and handing it back to me.

"Are you sure?" I asked, holding it up.

She nodded. "You do it."

I tore open the envelope, pulling out the letter and slowly reading it.

"Well?" she asked. So nervous.

I could have teased her that if it were that important she could have read it herself, but I didn't have the heart.

"They want you to audition. Next week."

She clapped her hands across her mouth, squealing before bursting into tears and averting her eyes downward.

"Maddy, what's wrong? This is good news, isn't it?"

She nodded slowly, still looking at the floor.

"Babe?"

"What if I get in?"

Her eyes were full of grief, as if something terrible had happened. I didn't understand.

"Isn't that what you want?"

She took a deep breath. "I thought it was. What if they want me to travel, go out of town? How do you manage work and Carly and everything here?"

I grabbed her hand, pulling her towards the couch. She sat on my lap, and I hugged her tight. "We'll do what we have to. This is your dream, and I would never stand in the way of that."

She frowned, burying her face in my neck, and we sat, rocking, until she found the words she was trying to say.

"I feel guilty, though. The thought of leaving you two. Carly's so little and you'd have to juggle so much, and ..."

I pushed her to sit up properly, cupping her face in my hands. "I owe you everything. You gave me my life back, made me live again. If I can help you live your dream, I'll do anything to make that happen."

Her chest heaved as she struggled to keep her composure, and I pressed my nose to hers, waiting until her breathing returned to normal.

"I'm sorry. I don't mean to get so wound up," she whispered.

I buried myself in her neck, her arms wrapped tight around mine. It wasn't her fault that she'd kept so much inside for all those years, trying to be strong and brave while her mother was bullied. Now I was there to be strong for her, and I needed her to understand that.

"Babe, this whole world is full of *what if*s. What if you ignore the one that changes your life?" I whispered.

Her grip loosened, and she leaned back to look at me, her eyes so tired and sad. "It's just so hard without Mum. She'll never get to see me if I make it, Andrew. I'm so scared that it'll happen and I can't share it with her. She missed so much, like Carly's birth."

I leaned my head on her breasts, breathing in her scent, so precious and so her. "She'll still share it, Maddy. Trust me; she'll know. She would be so proud of you right now, and if you follow your heart, that's all she could have ever hoped for. That's what I want for Carly, so it makes sense to want it for you too."

"You always know what I need to hear," she whispered, pressing her lips to the top of my head.

I stood, lifting her off the couch and grinning as she yelped in delight. "That's because we were just meant to be. Maybe you should trust yourself enough to take a leap of faith."

Maddy's eyes lit up, and I swung her around before setting her down on the floor. She chewed her bottom lip, taking my hands in hers, interlocking her fingers in mine.

"What are you up to?" I said, summoning the most innocent look I could muster.

"Taking you to bed to celebrate my decision to accept the audition offer."

"Really?" I squeezed her hands, moving forward until our faces were touching.

"Yes, really. Now, let's go do this before I get all soppy and start actually crying and stuff."

MADDY PRACTICED as much as she could right up to the day of her audition. She had her nagging doubts about the whole thing, and I knew it. But if she didn't at least try, she'd never know, and Carly and I gave her all the encouragement we could.

By the time the day of the audition came, she was a bundle of nerves and spent hours deciding what to wear.

"What do they want you to wear?" I asked, sitting on the bed, watching half her wardrobe contents falling to the floor.

"They didn't say. Do I dress formal, or what?"

"What do you want to do?"

She looked at me as if the thought hadn't occurred to her. "I'd feel more comfortable in my normal clothes."

"Well wear those then. If you're nervous about what you're wearing, it's not going to help."

She ran to the drawers, pulling out the denim skirt she was wearing when we met. "This has to be good luck," she said.

I shook my head, laughing. "Whatever you want, babe."

Maddy screwed up her face. "I wonder if I still fit it."

It was a little tighter than it used to be, but she pulled some leggings on underneath it. "Tada."

She gasped, a moment of inspiration hitting her as she returned to the drawer. Pulling out one of her mother's old Metallica T-shirts, she jumped up and down. It was a little baggy, but she smiled as she held out her arms.

I hugged her, stepping back to take another look. It was so Maddy, and somehow fitting.

"If they don't want me because I'm wearing this, they can go screw themselves." She laughed, full of the courage needed to face the audition now. They could take or leave her on her terms.

"That's my girl."

SHE EMERGED, pale as a ghost, as Carly and I waited in the lobby for her.

"Maddy? Are you okay?"

Her chest was rising and falling rapidly, and I reached for her arm, pulling her towards me. "Maddy?"

"I got in," she whispered.

"What?"

"I got in." She yelled this time, leaping up and wrapping her legs around my waist. She kissed me while I spun her around and Carly clapped and grabbed hold of my leg. My girls—my clever, beautiful girls.

"Let's go home and celebrate," she said, kissing me again.

I let her go, and she bent to pick up Carly, covering her face with kisses. "Mummy." Carly laughed, shaking her head.

"They've got a week of performances in a month's time and want me to play with them. It's a lot of practice, but so exciting," she said as we walked out together.

I squeezed her hand in mine, Carly holding onto my other hand.

Maddy, living her dream. I couldn't be more proud.

FORTY-FOUR

"SO, WHAT DO YOU THINK?" She appeared in the bedroom doorway in a white, collared blouse and ankle-length black skirt—the orchestral uniform.

I couldn't form words. It was similar to what she'd worn when she first met my parents, and memories of that night came flooding back. The night I knew I was in love with this beautiful woman. And she still obviously wore no underwear, the pink of her nipples showing as dark patches on her shirt.

"Andrew?"

I leapt out of bed, kneeling before her and gazing up at that gorgeous face. "You look amazing. One suggestion, though."

"What?"

I stood, cupping her breasts in my hands. "Wear a bra. I don't want anyone else looking at my property."

"Your what?" She laughed, my hands moving to her face to pull her in for a kiss. "Andrew." She gasped, running her hands down my back.

"I'm the only one that gets to see those." I stroked her nipples with my thumbs, bringing them to attention.

She shrugged. "It's a thick enough shirt. Only you would see."

"Oh, everyone would see, especially after I dump a bucket of cold water over your head."

Confusion crossed her face. "Why would you do that?"

"My own personal wet T-shirt competition." I waggled my eyebrows at her.

Maddy pressed her body against mine. "How cold would the water be?"

I ran my tongue up her neck, pausing to suck on an ear lobe. "Very cold. From the fridge."

She guided my hand around her back, low enough for me to realise she had no underwear on at all. I growled in her ear as she pressed harder against me.

"You know how hot I get when you talk about kitchen appliances," she whispered.

I picked her up, placing her on the bed on her back and began unbuttoning her shirt. If she had to wear it tomorrow night, it had to be in perfect condition. "Toasters," I said, after the first two buttons.

She laughed, closing her eyes and moaning as if the word had an affect on her.

"Food processor," I whispered, leaning over to kiss those perfect breasts, now uncovered.

"The bigger the appliance, the hotter I get," she murmured as I pulled her skirt down.

"Babe, your skirt might have gotten a bit wet," I said, nuzzling the soft hair between her legs.

"There's enough time to wash and dry my clothes before tomorrow. Pretty sure a bit of me isn't going to cause too much mess."

I kissed the tops of her thighs. "Washing machine," I said. Plunging my tongue into her, she wriggled, moaning for real this time.

Too hard to wait, I moved up her body, trailing kisses up towards her breasts, burying myself in her. "Clothes dryer." I waggled my eyebrows and she giggled, pulling me down to kiss her. She smelled so good, and I leaned in just to revel in that scent. Her eyes lit up as I thrust into her, and we moved together before I groaned, letting myself go.

"Vacuum cleaner," she murmured in a voice so sultry and seductive. I lost it, laughing so hard the bed shook.

"Love you, Maddy," I said once the moment had passed.

"I love you too. Even if you do have some weird obsession with appliances."

SHE WAS fast asleep at three o'clock when I put her clothes in the dryer. She would wake in the morning to find them clean and dry.

Curling up beside her, I snuggled in as tight as I could get. She stirred, before relaxing against me. Whatever fuelled her nervousness over this whole thing was gone, I hoped. It was as if she were frightened of being a success.

That she had found the courage to put herself forward for this made me so proud, and I drifted off to sleep with her in my arms, content with the world.

"Andrew! Where is it?" she screeched.

I sat up, rubbing my eyes as she pulled articles of clothing out of the drawers, flinging them about the room..

"What are you looking for?"

"My uniform. It was on the floor and I can't find it."

I laughed, shaking my head. "Clothes belong in the drawers, Maddy. Not on the floor."

"That's not helping." She stood, clutching a pair of jeans as she surveyed the room.

"I washed and dried it after you fell asleep last night. Your shirt and skirt are both in the dryer. Cool cycle, too, so they don't come out too wrinkled."

She leapt on the bed, pushing me back onto the pillow and closing my lips with hers. "Did I ever tell you how much I love you?" she asked, forgetting her irritation with me.

I laughed again. "I never get sick of hearing it, so you can tell me however many times you like. I know you're nervous. I wanted to help out."

We both jumped as the door flew open and Carly came running in, jumping on the bed.

"What are you doing, my little one?" Maddy asked her, laughing.

"We got a present for you. Daddy said I had to wait." She pouted, and Maddy's face lit up in surprise.

"A present?" Maddy asked, rolling off me, and pulling Carly into a hug.

"It was supposed to be for later," I said, screwing up my face at Carly.

She buried her head in her mother's neck. "Sorry."

"No point in holding back now. Hang on." I opened the top drawer of my bedside cabinet, and pulled out a small package. "Carly." I nudged her until she looked up at me, her little face lighting up at the sight of what I held. "Give this to your mother."

Maddy cocked an eyebrow at me as Carly handed her the box. Her jaw dropped as she opened it and saw what was inside.

"Carly saw it when we were out shopping last week. She recognised the symbol from your sheets of music," I said, watching Maddy turn the silver treble clef pendant over in her hand.

She smiled as she read the back. "*Good Luck. Love A and C.* I love it."

She leaned over Carly to kiss me before hugging Carly tight and kissing her. "I love you two so much. I'll make you proud tonight."

"We know you will," I said. Her eyes gleamed with happiness.

"With an awesome family like you guys, how can I not?"

"Mummy? Can we have breakfast now? I'm hungry." Carly sat up, her curls flopping all over her face.

Maddy grinned, that iridescent smile that always made my day.

"Of course." She tapped Carly on the nose. "Then, we go and brush that mop of hair. You have to look pretty tonight too."

Carly beamed. I loved watching the two of them together, the two loves of my life.

Today was going to be a pretty damn awesome day.

FORTY-FIVE

OUR LITTLE GROUP found its way to the seats set aside for us. Carly had special dispensation to be here, being Maddy's first public performance. They didn't normally allow children in for this type of performance.

She was also excited to have her grandparents there. Truth be told, I was sure she would have been content to stay home, basking in the attentions that Mum and Dad lavished on her, but this was a special night for all of us.

In the handful of years that Maddy and I had been together, I'd watched her grow into this woman who had the world at her fingertips. She'd always had that; she'd just never known it.

Rowan and Kyle sat on the other side of me, Rowan insisting on joining us for the evening. I think she was as proud of Maddy as I was, if that were possible. I knew she'd encouraged her to live her dream and shown my wife that she had gotten all she wanted while married with children. Her friendship had been a great boost to Maddy, even if she didn't want to admit she needed it.

We'd invited Bob, and Logan, but Bob wasn't one to be surrounded by people. Logan was buried in his own baby pooping and feeding fun. Listening to 'that classical crap' wasn't his thing either.

He had no idea what he was missing.

My stomach flipped as the curtain rose, and the strains of the orchestra starting their performance floated over the audience.

Carly tugged on my arm. "There's Mummy," she whispered. She climbed awkwardly onto my lap from her seat and I hugged her as she watched, bug-eyed, staring at her mother on stage. No one else was there as far as we were concerned, just Maddy, concentrating on her music and playing just as she was always meant to.

She shone, and it was as if I'd never seen her before, the sweet music she played causing me to fall in love with her all over again. Silence fell over the audience as they played.

"Mummy clever," Carly whispered in my ear, as enchanted as I was.

"She's very clever."

A hand landed on my arm, and I turned my head to see Rowan grinning, tears creeping into her eyes. I nodded, turning back to Carly and nuzzling the back of her neck. My beautiful baby was up there, playing her heart out, and I couldn't be any more proud.

As the music flowed into the next piece, Carly clapped and Maddy moved forward, playing her solo, eyes closed, feeling the music as it flew from her violin and over the audience. A grumpy-looking man in front of us turned to give us a filthy look. I just grinned back. "That's her mother," I said.

He gave me a faint smile, turning back to the music, and Maddy, my Maddy, won the crowd over with her talent, showing the world just how good she was.

And when she finished, the standing ovation told the six of us that we weren't the only ones feeling that way.

I STOOD, waiting for Maddy as people filed past me on the way out. Mum and Dad had already taken Carly home to bed, but I wanted some time with my wife before we drove home together.

So many random faces went past, but not the one I ached to see. The pride I felt for her made my chest ache, as if it were going to burst. Tonight her talent had shone so bright, and whatever accolades came now, she deserved every one.

Finally, she appeared at the door, a smile lighting her whole being as she stood and looked at me. She ran, flinging herself into my arms, and I spun her round. I had a flash of memory of that day in the park, Kyle doing the same to Rowan. This was how that felt, to take the woman who meant more to me than life itself in my arms and revel in the simplicity of just holding her and knowing she was mine.

"So?" she asked breathlessly.

"You were amazing," I said, kissing her and squeezing her tight.

"Not too tight." She laughed, nuzzling my nose with hers.

"I'm so proud of you. I hope you know that."

"I do," she whispered.

"Let's get going. Mum and Dad have taken Carly. I just want to go home to bed with you."

I let her go and she grinned at me, squeezing my arm.

"Maddy!" I heard a voice to my left and turned to see Rowan skip and grab hold of Maddy's arms. Kyle stood behind her, a smirk on his face.

"Hey." Maddy smiled, a quick glance up at me telling me she wanted out of here and for us to be alone. Just one glance.

"You were amazing. Hey, want to go grab something to eat with us? The kids are with Kyle's father, so we have a night off," Rowan babbled excitedly, but I knew Maddy's mind was elsewhere.

"That sounds great, but I'm exhausted and I still have four more nights to perform. Can we take a raincheck on that?"

Rowan's face fell. She could never hide her disappointment. "Of course. I didn't think about that. Maybe some other night. I'm so glad we came tonight, Maddy. It was fantastic."

"I think this will be the last of the late nights for a while for me, anyway. It'll be early nights every night for a few months after this."

I cocked an eyebrow, looking at her. "Yeah?"

"Well, if I get as tired as I did with Carly, I'll be getting a lot of sleep the next few weeks." Her eyes twinkled with mischief as she said the words, waiting for them to sink in.

"No way." Was she saying what I thought she was?

"Yes way. Playing with the orchestra has been the most amazing thing I think I've ever done, but it will have to take a back seat to a new baby."

I picked her up, swinging her around again, kissing her with abandon as people around us watched. We pressed our noses together. "Drama queen," I whispered.

"Did you expect anything different from me?" She laughed, pressing her lips to mine.

Rowan gasped. "Congratulations, Maddy. That's fantastic."

Kyle moved forward, wrapping his arms around Rowan from behind. "Let us get out of here, wife, and find some fun for ourselves." He winked at Maddy. "Great show, and congratulations."

He led Rowan away, and we waved as they disappeared into the distance. "I love them and everything, but I am glad to just be with you." Maddy leaned against me, and I slipped my arms around her waist.

"Me too, babe. Want to go somewhere and make out before we go home?"

She laughed, turning in my arms, hugging me tight. "As great as that sounds, I really do just want to go home. After we've gone through some drive-through on the way there and gotten something greasy to eat."

"Hey," I said, holding my arms out. "Now you're speaking my language."

MADDY and I stood in the doorway of Carly's room, watching her sleep. I'd reassembled the spare bed so Mum and Dad could stay, and they were already asleep. The house was so still and quiet.

"She's so beautiful," Maddy said.

"Just like her mother." I had my arms around Maddy, pulling her tight to me, never wanting to let go. "And soon we'll have a new one for me to worry about."

"We'll see. I'm not counting on anything until I know for sure that this baby will be okay. I'm sorry I announced it like that; it just seemed right." She smiled at me, and I bent my head to kiss her.

"Maddy, you wouldn't be you if you didn't do it in some dramatic fashion. Let's go to bed and celebrate." I rested my hand on her belly and closed my eyes.

Please let this one be okay.

"I'm scared," she whispered.

"Me too, but we'll find a way through this. Whatever happens, we'll be together and that's what matters."

I let her go, taking her hand and leading her to the bedroom.

I watched her sleep. We'd made love so slowly, so tenderly that she'd cried, and I'd held her as she let out her emotions. She was overwhelmed by the attention, by the baby, by our love.

Exhausted, she'd fallen asleep. Now, I watched her chest rise and fall, listened to each breath she took. My most precious thing.

Once again our life would take a different turn, an unexpected twist just when I thought we were on a steady path. As happy as I was at the thought of becoming a father again, I was terrified. Maddy couldn't take another blow. I didn't know if I could take another one.

It would be a long time before I felt I could breathe again.

FORTY-SIX

AUTUMN BROUGHT the change in weather, and our new child. Maddy gave birth to a boy at the start of the season.

"What are we going to call him?" Maddy asked. She'd been out of hospital a week, and neither of us had come up with a name.

"How about Robert?"

She smiled. Bob had been more of a father at times to her than her real father had. It seemed fitting to pass on the name.

"Robert. I like that. Bob will love it." He looked up at me with Maddy's eyes. Well, that's what he looked like he would end up with, those deep, dark pools that I just melted into.

"Andrew?" I turned my head to look at her. She screwed her mouth up as if unsure about what she had to say.

"What's wrong?"

Maddy broke out into a relieved smile. "You always did know how to read me."

"I can see you're worried about something. What is it?"

She lowered her eyes. "I don't think I want another baby. I mean, we have two beautiful, healthy children, and I'm scared we'd be tempting fate to try again."

I ran my finger down her cheek, lifting her chin so her gaze was fixed on me. "I agree. I know we talked about having more, but that was before you ended up having surgery. We're so blessed. I'm blessed to have you and the kids. I can't ask for anything more."

She clung onto me, her arms tight around my waist, gazing at our son in my other arm. "He's so beautiful."

"He is, just like his big sister, and just like his mother."

"You always have been good for my ego." Maddy poked her tongue at me.

I disentangled myself, passing Robert to her. "I need to go and cook dinner."

Carly looked up at me, her eyes shining with excitement. "Can I have chicken nuggets?"

Maddy and I laughed. "I'm pretty sure I can manage that," I said.

"Shame I won't get the benefits of that," Maddy muttered.

"Plenty of time to catch up." I laughed. Tiny limbs waved at me as Robert managed to work himself out of my useless swaddling attempt.

"Aww sweetie. Let Mummy wrap you up properly, seeing as Daddy is just so hopeless." Maddy grinned up at me as I walked to the door.

"Totally hopeless."

Wouldn't have it any other way.

BY THE TIME WINTER CAME, Rowan was pregnant. She and Maddy were as thick as thieves, as Maddy threw herself into supporting her friend. The mistakes of the past weren't forgotten, but we all put them aside to get on with our lives. Our children adored each other, and I often watched Carly with Mia and Charlie, thinking of the old days with my Charlie and Rowan.

Kyle and I would always have a barrier between us, the one I put up. While that would never completely fall, we broke a hole through it, finding a way to co-exist while our wives giggled and gossiped. It helped that we adored them, the amazing women we had chosen to spend our lives with.

Sometimes, I heard Charlie's laugh, carried by the wind. It made me feel warm, loved, and I missed her more than ever.

Then I heard Maddy. If ever there was anyone else meant for me, it was her. We were so in sync it was frightening, and I still looked back on that day in the park with Rowan and the love between her and Kyle that was so clear to see. That was us. Maddy and me—forever.

Carly was next. Clone of my wife, the little girl who helped bring Maddy closer to me, who gave meaning to my life when I had so little. I'd walk to the ends of the earth for that girl, and it still wouldn't be enough to show her how much she meant to me.

My little miracle, Robert. He'll never really understand just how precious he is. Our last child, my son. We'll never have another. But we're happy with our pigeon pair, and nothing in the world will ever top their births.

After work, I pulled into the driveway, and it was always the same routine. A delighted chorus of "Daddy" and my babies were in my arms, tugging at me for my attention, tugging at my heart. Behind them, Maddy usually stood, bemused, eyes full of love. I could live to be a million and never get sick of that look.

And in the evening, when the children were in bed, Maddy and I continued our love story, the one that began on the stairs.

The one that would never end.

ALSO BY WENDY SMITH

Coming Home

Doctor's Orders

Baker's Dozen

Hunter's Mark

Teacher's Pet

A Very Campbell Christmas

Fall and Rise Duet

Falling

Rising

Fall and Rise - The Complete Duet

The Aeon Series

Game On

Build a Nerd

Bar None

Hollywood Kiwis Series

Common Ground

Even Ground

Under Ground

Rocky Ground

Coming soon Solid Ground

Stand alones

For the Love of Chloe

Only Ever You

The Friends Duet
Loving Rowan
Three Days

The Forever Series
Something Real
The Right One
Unexpected

Chances Series
Another Chance
Taking Chances

Lifetime Series
In a Lifetime
In an Instant
In a Heartbeat
In the End
At the Start

ABOUT THE AUTHOR

Wendy Smith is a multi-platform bestselling author, whose book In the End, written as Ariadne Wayne, was named one of Apple's best books of 2017. She lives with her two children and two cats in New Zealand where she bases her books because she loves living there. All her stories come with a quirky sense of humour, and she cries over everything.

Find me online
www.wendysmith.co.nz
wendy@wendysmith.co.nz